ONE *Kiss*

ALEATHA ROMIG
NEW YORK TIMES BESTSELLING AUTHOR

A Riverbend Lighter One

A small-town, best-friend's-sister, age-gap, grumpy, sunshine, 'lighter' ONE stand-alone contemporary romance

ALEATHA ROMIG

New York Times, Wall Street Journal, and USA Today bestselling author

Blurb

One Kiss

A small-town, best-friend's-sister, age-gap, grumpy, sunshine, contemporary stand-alone

Confirmed bachelor—that's what I've become.

Life is safe and predictable. After all, Riverbend doesn't exactly have a roaring social life or an influx of women looking to be the wife of a farmer.

Hold on.

I'm not looking for a wife—or even a girlfriend.

When my best friend tells me that his little sister, Devan, is moving back to Riverbend to teach science, I envision the little girl with pigtails, freckles, and an annoying urge to be wherever her older brother was. Of course, that was twelve years ago when she was ten years old.

Newsflash. Devan is no longer a child.

Imagine my shock when I learn that she is the woman who disappeared after one passionate kiss—one I couldn't get out of my head.

Once I realize Devan is my mystery woman, I can't walk away.

The problem is that she's my best friend's little sister, ten years younger than I am, and definitely off-limits.

What will it mean for my friendship if I pursue my feelings?
Can one kiss change everything?
Have you been Aleatha'd?

ONE KISS is a stand-alone, age-gap, best-friend's-sister, small-town, forbidden contemporary romance set in Riverbend, Indiana, and one of Aleatha's Lighter Ones. Sit back and enjoy the hijinks as Justin's safe and predictable world is turned upside down.

Chapter One

Devan

Letting out a long breath, I plop down on the couch in our apartment and sigh. Marilyn, my best friend and roommate shakes her head.

"Hmm," I say.

Marilyn starts to laugh. "You know, you could just talk without all the drama and sound effects."

"What fun would that be?"

Marilyn and I have been friends since before kindergarten. Neither one of us resembles the little girls we were. Well, there are subtle similarities. Her dark chocolate hair and bright blue eyes. My blond hair and light brown eyes. However, the differences are evident. While her DD cup is much larger than my B cup, we've both grown up. And through it all, we are there for one another.

Our first period.

Our first kiss.

Our first date.

Our first heartbreak.

Graduation.

College.

Everything.

Marilyn sets her phone on the side table and plucks the earbuds from her ears. "Okay, Drama Devan, spill."

"I got a call from Mr. Sams."

"He called you? What is wrong with people from Riverbend? Don't they know that no one calls anymore? It's all text messages or email."

Marilyn knows my hometown because it's her hometown too. We both left after high school graduation, dusting the dirt from our shoes—or something like that—and vowing to move on to bigger and better places.

It's not that Riverbend is bad.

It's just Riverbend.

The same town where my grandparents lived, and my parents and brother live. It's a town that is the same as it was when I was in grade school, middle school, and high school. Now, the middle-school principal called me about an opening for a seventh-grade teacher. Seeing as I'm about to graduate with my education degree, a job is something I need.

"I know. Right?" I nibble on my lower lip. "Mr. Sams is *Cory* Sams." I say his name that way because when we were in grade school, he was in high school. And we both thought he was dreamy.

Marilyn nods. "Did I give you my undivided attention so you could take me through the Riverbend phone book?"

"Oh God. Do you think they still have a phone book?"

My friend laughs. "I'm not sure about the phone book. Yes, I know who Mr. Sams is. He's your brother's friend. I remember when all those guys would hang out at your house."

I think back to that time. Nearly ten years younger than my brother, Ricky, I was always the pesky little sister.

"Do you think," Marilyn asks, "that Mr. Sams knows you're Ricky's *little* sister?" The way she says little is drawn out, emphasizing the age gap.

"Seeing as my last name is Dunn, the same as my brother's, I would say yes. Besides he started the conversation with small talk. All professional yet friendly." I shrugged. "He knows."

"You had an interview for Indianapolis schools, too. Didn't you say it went well?"

Grabbing a throw pillow, I hug it in front of me. "Maybe I should be like you and go straight to grad school." I could do that. If I wanted to take on more debt. My parents are as helpful as they can be, but I know that money is tight. I won't be the reason they struggle.

Marilyn smiles. "And we could stay roommates. You

could pay half the rent." Her blue eyes open wide. "If you take the job in Riverbend, you can live at home." She shakes her head at my eye roll. "I know. Think about the money you'd save."

"That's why I haven't told Mom about the interview. I was thinking maybe you'd go with me, and we could stay at your parents' or get a room somewhere. It's springtime. There might be something happening."

"First, it's Little 500 weekend. There are no rooms to be had anywhere near Bloomington."

"Oh. I didn't think of that." My smile grows. "That means there are probably parties in Bloomington. That campus is a lot wilder than Ball State."

Marilyn rolls her eyes. "Of course, there are parties. Since when are you the partying type?"

"Since I'm hoping to fly under the radar in Riverbend. I don't want anyone to know that I'm considering the position."

"You think you could get into town and no one will know? Devan, this is Riverbend you're talking about. I'd be surprised if Janet isn't already picking out paint for your bedroom in anticipation of your return."

Laying my head against the cushions, I stare up at the ceiling. "That's Mom." Another nibble of my lip and I move my gaze to my best friend. "Am I failing if I go back?"

"No," she answers quickly. "You have nailed your classes. And your student teaching earned you multiple job offers."

I spent last semester student teaching in Muncie, north of Indianapolis, in an accelerated private academy. I took the assignment because Marilyn and I both live in Muncie, attending Ball State University. Despite the funny name, it's one of the best education colleges around.

"I've thought about it," I say. "You're moving to Bloomington for grad school and" —I think about our core group of friends— "everyone is moving somewhere. I guess I don't want to be left here without my friends."

"Indianapolis?"

"Ricky would tell me I'm being a baby, but the thing is, Indy is big. Bigger than Muncie and a lot bigger than Riverbend. The school system is huge, and from what I've read, underfunded. It seems like a lot of stress for my first job, worrying about where to live, lesson plans, and supplies."

"When is your interview with Mr. Sams?"

My lips curl as I dip my chin, bat my eyelashes, and send my friend my most pleading expression. "Tomorrow."

"Tomorrow? You know I have an eight a.m. facilitator group.

"You're a senior. Who does that themselves?"

"Someone who's trying to ace advanced calculus." She grins. "And the TA in the Friday morning discussion is worth waking up for."

"And I thought it was all about you being an over-achiever," I say.

"Says Miss Straight As."

My smile fades.

"Hey, that's not a bad thing," Marilyn says. "It's amazing. You should be proud."

"It's that drive that makes me think accepting a job back in Riverbend is taking the easy way out. And I'm not an easy-way-out person. You know that. I love a challenge."

"Don't overthink it. I'll go to Riverbend with you tomorrow after discussion. What time is the interview?"

"It's not until four, after school is out."

"We'll have plenty of time. I'll call Mom and tell her it's a covert operation, one requiring the utmost secrecy."

Marilyn's dramatization makes me laugh. "I love it. And I'll text Jill." She's a classmate from Riverbend who is a senior at IU. "She'll know if there's anything happening to get us out of Riverbend on a Friday night."

"You don't have to take the job."

Lifting the pillow to my chest, I smile. "I'm afraid I'll want it."

"Devan, your eyes are sparkling. Why are you fighting this?"

"Because I never wanted to end up in Riverbend...an RTS." It's a local term for people who leave and return—return to sender. "I mean what will I become, the quintessential old spinster schoolteacher for the rest of my life?"

"You're twenty-two years old. I think it's a little early to be worried about that."

"There's no one in Riverbend. They're all married, moved away, gay, or worse, like Ricky."

Marilyn shrugs. "Your brother is a dick, but I guess he's all rugged sexy."

"Eww. He's not. He's a hard worker. My dad farmed. Ricky farms. The last thing I want to be is a farmer's wife."

"All that hard work builds muscles." Her eyebrows dance.

More laughs bubble from my throat. "It also causes some serious stink." I wave my hand in front of my nose. "Serious."

Chapter Two

Justin

"Do you ever feel like we're the odd men out?" my friend Ricky Dunn asks.

"Out of what?"

Shaking his head, Ricky leans back, causing his chair to teeter on two legs. There's a piece of grass between his teeth, dangling like an unlit cigarette. The view before us is of the Dunn farm. It's about the same acreage as the Sheers farm—mine. Officially, it still belongs to my parents, but the time is coming sooner rather than later when Dad will be done. His health hasn't been perfect and honestly, it's damn hard work keeping a farm going, staying in the black. I'm not talking profitable. I'm talking about keeping our heads above water.

I'm the first in our area to investigate selling corn to a company in Illinois. My brother-in-law has taken the idea further and is working to get more of our seed corn to be made into ethanol. He's a fancy-assed lawyer who finally got his head out of his ass. It's a long story, but right now, he's living the dream in Riverbend.

That's it—Ricky's question.

I turn to my friend. "You're talking about wives and kids."

Ricky nods. "Judy and Cory's new boy is here. That gives them two. Mick and Chloe's kid is what...two years old?"

I shrug. "The kid is walking. What age does that happen?" Okay, I'm not exactly clueless. I was around a lot when my niece Molly was little. Now that she's living in town with her parents, I get to be a regular uncle—not someone she sees every day, and honestly, it kind of sucks. I miss that little girl.

Ricky brings his chair forward, the front legs slamming against the porch floor. He lowers his voice. "Fuck, I thought this would be what I'd do forever."

There is something in his tone. "And what the fuck are you planning to do?"

"Dad is talking about selling the farm."

"No," I say resolutely. "To who?"

"That developer, you know the new subdivision south of town?"

My skin tightens as I stand to my feet. My mud-caked boots leave a trail on the porch floor. "No," I repeat. "Fuck no. Five hundred acres of your land border ours. I'm not having stupid McMansions next to my fields. Those whiners say they want country living until they're stuck behind a tractor doing twenty in a fifty-five. Or during harvesting, when dust flies through their open windows." I have an idea. "Sell it to me."

"You don't have that kind of capital."

"I'm a thirty-two-year-old who lives with his parents." I gesture toward the driveway. "I've been driving the same truck for over seven years." Hell yeah. It's a damn good truck. I shrug. "Tell Jack to talk to me. I'll even bring Dax in on it if I have to."

Ricky shakes his head. "I don't want him to sell to anyone, but I get it."

"Have you told him?"

"Oh, we've had a few good discussions about it."

"Your mom?" I ask, wondering what my mom would say if Dad ever thought about selling our land.

"She thinks Devan will stay gone after college."

"Yeah," I answer, "but she's what, a sophomore?"

Ricky chuckles. "She's a senior, asshole."

"Oh, forgive me for not keeping up-to-date on your little sister."

"I know that Kandace and Dax are expecting."

Kandace is my sister. Of course, he knows. She's here.

"They live in Riverbend. Hell, the news got out right after he knocked her up again. Devan left and I still imagine her with pigtails, freckles, and the annoying need to be wherever we were."

That makes Ricky laugh. "Well, if Devan stays in

Muncie or moves to Indy, Mom is talking about going somewhere warm. She says she's sick of Indiana winters."

Turning I look my friend up and down. "What about you? This is what you do."

"Maybe I should consider doing something else. Look at Mick, Cory, and Dax. They have real jobs and get to play farmer on weekends. It might be nice not to look at a field soaked in spring rain and calculate the loss of wheat."

I suck in a breath. I know exactly what he's talking about. We were both doing it today. That's why both of our pairs of boots are caked in mud. The wheat should be ready to harvest in a few weeks. The rain over the last few days is messing with the fields. Shit, there are now lakes where there used to be crop. If the fields don't dry up soon, we won't be running tractors out there. "Talk to Jack. I'm serious. Give me a chance to buy. Dad and I can probably do it, but if we bring Kandace and Dax in on it, it's a sure thing."

"You don't know what that developer is offering."

"I don't care," I say with determination. "We're neighbors. And I hate to play the card, but you're my best friend."

"Only because everyone else is married and too busy for you."

Laughing, I shake my head. "There might be something to that."

Inhaling, Ricky stands. "The Gordons are having their annual hog roast Friday night. Are you going?"

"Kandace said she and Dax are going to be there. I'm not sure I'm up for a town gathering to hear about more kids on the way."

"Then go for the great food and you know, there's always a few kegs."

I nod and look at my watch. "I need to head home. See you tomorrow at breakfast?"

"Damn right. One of the few times the guys can break away from their ball and chain."

That makes me smile. I never thought of my sister as a ball and chain, but in that scenario she is. I take the porch steps down to the path, heading toward where my truck is parked. Turning, I take in the Dunn house. It's a lot like the one where I live. It's old and big and home. I spent many nights there when we were younger. It isn't new or filled with the latest technology. I can't fathom thinking about this house or mine being torn down to make small cookie-cutter houses. "Ricky," I call out, "tell Jack I'm serious."

"Shouldn't you talk to Randy and Dax first?"

"We might not all be on the same page all the time, but when it comes to Riverbend, we are. I don't want to see the farmland disappear."

"Some call that progress."

"Yeah," I say, "I'm not one of those."

Chapter Three

Devan

I flop down on Marilyn's childhood bed the way I've done a thousand times. Staring around her room, I see that nothing has changed. The same posters Marilyn tacked up on her walls during high school are still present. I giggle at the sight of Mumford & Sons, remembering what a great time we had at that concert.

The door opens and my best friend comes inside. "I can't tell if you're happy about the interview or sad."

Propping myself up on my elbows, I smile. "I think I'm both."

"What does that mean?" she asks, sitting on the side of the full-size mattress.

Moving until I'm sitting with my legs crisscrossed, I let myself think about the next step. You know. Moving on, being an adult. It's scary, and I'm gravitating toward the idea of letting it happen in a place where I'm comfortable. "No matter which job I take, the students will call me Miss Dunn. Isn't that crazy?"

Marilyn laughs. "I think that's the way it works."

I scrunch my nose. "Seventh graders are like twelve and thirteen years old. I'm only twenty-two. It's weird."

"Nine to ten years is a lot." She wiggles her shoulders. "I can see it now. I bet all the boys will have a crush on Miss Dunn."

"Not if I teach in Riverbend and they know of Ricky. He was my worst nightmare when it came to guys when I was young. They were all scared of him."

Marilyn lies down on the bed and turns toward me, holding her head in her hand with her elbow on the bedspread. "That's why you didn't date much in high school. What's your excuse for college?"

"I date. I guess." Not a lot, but I've gone out. Shrugging, I assess. "Maybe I'm not datable material."

Her eyes open wide. "Are you joking? Have you looked at yourself lately? You're gorgeous. And not only that, but you're also fun to be around. Otherwise, I wouldn't have put up with you for the last four years."

My smile turns to a pout. "I'm going to miss you."

With her lips in a straight line, Marilyn nods. Our separation at the end of this semester is the giant elephant in the room. We both have plans even if mine aren't set yet.

Before we can get all mushy and emotional, the door

swings open, and our friend Jill appears. "I'm here," she announces.

The room echoes with our screams as Marilyn and I scramble off the bed and we all hug. Yes, there's a bit of jumping too. The three of us were inseparable throughout our childhood. And if you ask me, Jill was always the most beautiful. Her auburn hair and green eyes make her eye-catching. But just like what Marilyn said about me, it's Jill's outgoing personality that makes her special. We were the good girls with good grades who got away with too much talking.

"I'm so glad you two came back this weekend," Jill says. "I can't take another Little 500 weekend in Bloomington." She shakes her head, her long hair swinging across her back, and scrunches her nose. "I'd much rather spend the weekend here with the two of you."

Softly, I push against her shoulder. "I didn't tell anyone else we came to town. I was hoping to escape Riverbend and go to Bloomington. You know, check out the fun."

Throwing her big bag on Marilyn's bed, she takes a seat beside it. "At IU, Little 500 is amateur weekend. The parties are mostly filled with underclassmen." Shaking her head, she adds, "Unless you're imagining a night that ends with walking through puke, I suggest we come up with something better."

"Eww," Marilyn and I say together.

"Way to paint a disgusting word picture," I say.

Jill lowers her chin while watching the two of us

from behind veiled lashes. "I have something to tell you two, and before you get mad...I was waiting to see you in person."

As her words come faster and faster, Marilyn and I look at one another and back to Jill.

"Oh my God," Marilyn says. "You're pregnant."

Jill snickers and shakes her head.

"You got a job?" I ask.

"A summer one," she answers. "My other news is more exciting."

"What?" we both practically scream.

She lifts her left hand, revealing a modest yet pretty diamond.

Marilyn and I scream again as we rush toward her, tackling her as the room fills with laughter, oohs, ahs, and congratulations.

"I can't believe Todd proposed," I say, thinking out loud about how Jill and Todd have been an item since our sophomore year of high school. Well, he was a senior, and let me say, Jill's mom, Suzy, wasn't a fan. Luckily for Todd, Jill doesn't have an intimidating older brother.

With all three of us sitting on the bed, Jill is nodding fast, and her smile is so big it spans the width of her face. "He asked me two weeks ago."

"Two weeks," Marilyn says, "and you didn't tell us."

She holds her left hand out and wiggles her fingers. The diamond glitters under the light. "It wasn't something to tell my two best friends in a text or on Snapchat."

I imagine receiving that text. She's right, we would have been happy for her, but tackling her in person is better.

"How did he do it?"

"Do you have a date?"

"Which one of us is your maid of honor?"

We sling questions right and left.

"We went out to dinner in Indy" —she absolutely beams— "and after dinner, he suggested we go to the Circle for dessert. I love the South Bend Chocolate Company. Anyway, on the steps in front of the monument, he fell to one knee." She brings her hands to her chest. "I started crying."

It was probably a given that Jill would marry first, but at the same time, it's hard to wrap my head around.

Married.

With a husband.

She'll be a wife.

Jill goes on, "We're thinking next summer. So, a year away. Todd will be done with his MBA."

"What about your grad school?" I ask.

"I've applied to IUPUI. Todd lives in Indy, and now I'm moving in with him." She looks at me. "Tell me that you're taking the teaching job in Indy."

I shrug. "I haven't made a decision."

"Devan got another offer," Marilyn says, her eyebrows dancing.

"Wait. What?" Jill asks as she reaches for my hand. "I didn't know you were even dating."

"No," I say, "not that kind of offer. Teaching. I had an interview today."

Her forehead furrows. "Today? Before you got to Riverbend?"

Pressing my lips together, I shake my head.

Jill's green eyes open wide. "Oh, here." She hops off the bed. "Devan Dunn is moving back to Riverbend."

"It's not official," I say. "I'm torn. Especially now that I know you'll be in Indy."

Her green eyes sparkle. "You do what is best for you. I'd love to live close, but if you come back here, Marilyn will still be in Bloomington, right between us. We can meet up there. And you can keep us up-to-date on all things in Riverbend."

Marilyn's eyes squint. "You just said that you don't like being in Bloomington."

"On Little 500 weekend. Trust me, there are plenty of nice grown-up, puke-free places to have a good time any other weekend of the year."

Standing, I turn a circle and shake my head. "Oh my God," I say, struck with the realization that it isn't only happening to me. "You guys..."

They both turn my way.

"We are really grown-ups." I scrunch my nose. "Aren't we?"

"Not too fast," Marilyn says. She turns to Jill. "Is Todd coming to Riverbend this weekend?"

"Nope. I told him I wanted some time with the two of you." She rolls her eyes. "He's insanely busy with his classes. I'll head to Indy on Sunday and probably back to Bloomington Monday before class."

Marilyn grins. "I'm curious if Mrs. Kohlberg is aware of your plans."

"Mom's excited about the engagement. She may or may not know I visit Indy regularly."

We all laugh.

"Okay," I say. "We order pizza and hang out in Marilyn's bedroom, or we go do something."

"Something," Marilyn says with a smile looking around the room.

"Ideas?" I ask.

Jill responds, "Todd reminded me that tonight is the Gordons' hog roast."

"No," I answer. "Remember, my visit is covert."

"I forgot." Jill grins. "I have an idea. We wait until it gets dark." She opens Marilyn's closet and starts looking through her things. Jill pulls out a Purdue hoodie from when Marilyn's older brother Marcus went to Purdue. "And we go incognito. We can spy on our old classmates, see what's happening that our moms haven't told us."

Rolling my eyes, I say, "It will only be old people and people who never broke free."

Jill stands her ground. "You know this hog roast is always a big deal, remember? We even went in high school. It's the first party of the year, getting people out after the long winter. I think it's pretty cool Mrs. Gordon is carrying it on after Mr. Gordon died. And some people have broken free but want to come back. Am I looking at one of those?"

Is she?

I don't know.

Marilyn nudges me with her elbow. "Might be a good way to explore your thoughts about moving back."

I take the hoodie from Jill's grasp. "And you think wearing a sweatshirt from another school will fake out the people we've known all our lives?" I make eye contact with one friend and then the other, seeing the sparkle from both. "Okay, let's do this!"

"Can you find two more sweatshirts?" Jill asks Marilyn.

"Are you kidding? My parents have enough Purdue and Ball State attire to clothe a small country."

I pull the hoodie over my head.

It's at least three sizes too big, and the hem lands in the middle of my thighs. Moving the hood over my head, I step in front of the full-length mirror. A genuine laugh bubbles out of me as I take in my reflection. "Oh right. Add darkness and sunglasses and it might work."

Jill laughs. "Since it will be dark, we should probably skip the glasses."

"Yes, and it will be after dark," Marilyn says. "This will be fun. Just like old times."

"If anyone asks," I say, still looking at my reflection, "my name is Echo."

"Echo?"

I shrug. "I just made it up. Seriously, my mom would

be upset if she knew I came to town and didn't tell her. I don't want to hurt her feelings."

"Did you hear someone?" Jill asks Marilyn.

They both laugh. "Not someone. I think it was an echo."

Chapter Four

Justin

I swing my seven-year-old niece into my arms as her giggles fill my ears.

"Uncle Justin," she squeals as her little arms wrap around my neck for only a second before she wriggles to be put down.

As soon as her feet hit the ground, she's running to an area farther away from the bonfire, one dominated by people her size. She is completely in her element, playing with friends she's known most of her life. I suppose it's not a lot different than those I'm standing with—friends forever. A hand comes to my lower back. I turn, seeing my sister's smile.

"Remember when she wanted to be held all the time?"

"Yeah."

Kandace hands me a plastic cup with foam.

"Since when do you bring me beer?"

"Apparently, not everyone in Riverbend knows everything." She laughs. "Crystal brought it to me. Hated to see it go to waste."

"You mean, she doesn't know about" —my gaze goes to Kandace's midsection and back to Kandace's blue eyes, a little lighter than my own— "my new niece or nephew? Shocker."

The truth is that Kandace isn't showing yet. That doesn't usually stop the gossip mill.

"I know," she says. "Riverbend needs to up its game. It's not like Dax and I have announced it formally or on social media, but come on, this is Riverbend."

I take a sip of the beer. "Dax tell you about the Dunns' farm." I wasn't sure if it was a question. The thing is that I've been giving the whole concept a lot of thought.

Kandace nods. "I'm pretty sure," she whispers, "it's not something we should talk about here—especially if they aren't sure about selling."

"You're probably right."

She bumps my shoulder with hers. "What's eating you?"

Kandace knows me well. I've felt off since Ricky told me about the possible sale. "Nothing," I lie.

"Yeah, right." She looks all around. "In case you'd like to inform your face, you're at a party, the kickoff of spring. Tradition."

My lips quirk to a smirk. "I like tradition. It's change I don't care for."

"There's my brother. Admit what bugs you and try smiling. I promise it won't hurt."

My cheeks rise as I shake my head. "You can be a real pain in the ass."

Kandace laughs loud enough for others to look our direction. I take another drink of the beer.

"Thanks for helping me out," she says with a wink and a glance at the cup.

"I've got your back. Bring me all the beer."

Soon we're joined by her husband, Dax. Before I know it, Cory and Judy Sams and Mick and Chloe Reynolds are also here. The conversation goes from the recent rain to the upcoming softball season. Of course, there are mentions of children.

We aren't the only group talking, laughing, and drinking—well, other than my sister on the last one. Across the open lawn, Mom and Dad are talking with Lynell Jacobs and his wife. This hog roast is truly a Riverbend tradition.

Kandace and Dax move to the stadium chairs they brought.

With the sun below the horizon, there's a chill to the spring air. The cooling temperature doesn't stop the fun as more and more cars pull onto the farm, parking near the big barn. Headlights stream across the crowd and go dark. There are three long tables filled to overflowing with dishes everyone brought. Since I live with Mom and

Dad, I didn't need to contribute. Mom brought enough potato salad and green bean casserole for an army. Nevertheless, I'm a grown man.

I brought a bag of potato chips.

A giant bag.

The kind with ridges.

Leaving the married couples to themselves, I make my way over to the keg. While a lot of the men in this cluster are younger than me, some are also older. I pick up on my dad's discussion.

"Yeah, I know it's a slow start, but the Cardinals will pull themselves up. I see a pennant in the future."

"Distant future," Ricky says. He and my dad have always razzed one another about baseball. Ricky was raised a Red Sox fan. It's stupid with him living his whole life in Indiana. I've heard the story. It's that Ricky's dad, Jack, is left-handed. When he was a kid, he was given a Fred Lynn autographed left-handed glove. Fred was a center fielder for the Red Sox. The rest is history. Not only for Jack but for the next generation as well.

Peering over the rim of Dad's cup, I grin, seeing the pink of the lemonade available near the food table. Dad has had a few health problems and not drinking alcohol is one of the ways he's working to keep himself healthy.

After a detailed analysis of the Cardinals' pitching lineup, I decide to take a walk. I'm not sure exactly what's eating at me. It could be the idea of the Dunns selling. Whatever it is, my skin is too tight and even a cup of beer doesn't ease my taut nerves.

I know the Gordon property like I know my own. The Gordon farm is bigger, at least by four times. There isn't a man in Riverbend who hasn't at one time worked on this farm. Not always for money. That's the way things are around here. We pitch in. At harvest time, even people who live away come back to help.

Well, it's tradition.

Like tonight's party.

My boots slip in the soft mud as I make my path away from the crowd of people and the orange glow of the bonfire. With each step, the voices dull and the sky above me grows blacker, the stars multiply, and the moon shows itself near the horizon.

Big.

Round.

Bright.

Stuffing my hands into the pockets of my jacket, I stand at the top of a ridge. The large barn and party are behind me. Ahead of me is a pond surrounded by what will soon be fields filled with hay. A smile curls my lips as I recall swimming in that murky water of the pond as a kid. Probably everyone did. How we didn't come out covered in leeches, I'll never know.

Something catches my eye.

No.

Not something.

Someone.

Up ahead near the pond, I see a slender figure.

Is that person wearing a cape?

What the hell?

This isn't a costume party.

Steadying my steps so I don't slip, I go closer to the pond. My ears perk up, but all I hear is the distant party and the sounds of an Indiana night. The chirping crickets are a sure sign the weather is warming.

As I get closer, I see that it's not a cape the person is wearing but a hooded sweatshirt. With the rising of the moon, I can tell the color is golden. From the size of the person, I'm assuming it's a woman. "Are you all right?" I ask.

The person spins.

The moonlight brightens her face.

She's definitely a woman.

Damn.

Her eyes are as big as saucers.

"You scared me," she says in a friendly yet frightened tone.

I lift my hands. "Sorry." Reading her sweatshirt, I add, "Boiler up."

"What?" She looks down and laughs. "Right. Yes. Boiler up."

Her laugh is contagious, and for a moment I join in.

Tilting my head, I walk closer. With each step I realize how petite this woman is. Nevertheless, with my eyes on hers, I have no doubt she's a grown woman. "Are you from around here?"

She pushes her hands in the front pocket of her sweatshirt. "I used to be."

Shaking my head, I stop a few feet away. "I'm sure I'd remember you if you still lived here." I gesture back to the party. "How did you hear about this? It's kind of a local thing."

"A friend invited me."

"Oh." I look around. "Is that friend going to be upset that I'm talking to you?" I don't know what's come over me. I'm not usually this forward. Then again, I meant to get away from people, not come face-to-face with an attractive woman.

She pushes the hood off her head.

My breath catches as the moonlight glistens off her light hair. It's piled on top of her head in what Kandace calls a messy bun. Even messy she's stunning. With a perky nose, full pink lips, and a slender neck, I'm awestruck.

"I don't have a boyfriend or significant other—if that's what you're asking."

"I don't know how that is possible."

Her chin lowers.

The movement is shy, cute, and damn sexy.

"My name is Justin."

Chapter Five

Devan

Holy shit. This is Justin Sheers.

I recognize him, but he obviously doesn't recognize me.

"Hi, Justin," I say, unwilling to give away my identity.

With his hands pushed down in the pockets of his jeans, I see the man my brother's friend has become. His auburn hair is mussed—not short but not too long. His chiseled jaw is covered by a day's or more beard growth showing red even by the light of the moon. It's his eyes, though, that I can't look away from.

When did they become so intense?

The blue shimmers.

I take a step closer, unsure if I'm imagining this encounter. Maybe it's my subconscious giving me another reason to consider Riverbend. As the thought comes, it goes. Once Justin Sheers knows who I am, he won't be interested in me.

"Are you all right?" he asks with a sexy grin. "A moment ago, you were smiling, and now you're not."

Swallowing, I consider my next words.

He takes a step closer. As I look up, I can smell the scent of bodywash, the aroma of the bonfire, and the beer on his breath. My heart beats faster as butterflies come to life in my stomach. Never have I had this reaction to mere presence. This is crazy.

This is Justin Sheers.

His touch comes to my chin. It's warm, soft in a gentle way, yet coarse, the hands of a working man. I forget to breathe as he lifts my chin to resume our eye contact.

"You have a beautiful smile."

His voice is like his touch—deep and soothing while at the same time, abrasive in a way that twists my core and tightens my nipples. I say a quick prayer, thanking God that I'm wearing the oversized sweatshirt.

"Thank you," I finally manage to say. It was an octave too high, but I made the words go out.

Blinking, he lets go of my chin and taking a step back, shakes his head. "I'm sorry."

"For what?"

"I'm not a creep or some perv."

My cheeks rise. "I wasn't thinking you were."

A sparkle returns to his gaze. "There's that smile."

Inhaling, I confess. "It's been a while since I've been back to Riverbend and that" —I lift my chin to the distant sounds of the growing party— "is a bit overwhelming."

"I get it. I live here day in and day out, and it is overwhelming."

"I'm sure," I say, "you know everyone at the party."

Justin shrugs. "I thought I did." His smile returns. "I don't. You haven't told me your name."

Closing my eyes, I carry on my internal debate, the one I've been having with myself since Justin introduced himself. I could introduce myself as Echo, but I don't want to lie to him. I also don't want to be truthful. As the argument rages in my head, Justin again reaches for my chin. When my eyes open, he's close, very close.

"If you don't tell me your name, I can't ask you if I can kiss you."

I swallow. "You want to kiss me?"

"It's all I've been thinking about since you took off the hood."

"Why?"

His smile grows and a laugh fills the air. "I can't think of anything to say that won't sound cheesy, and if you knew me, you'd know I'm not a cheesy person." Releasing my chin, he steps back and takes off his jacket. It's a Carhartt—tan on the outside with lining on the inside. Justin lays the coat on the soft ground. "Would you like to sit?"

Nodding, I sit to one side of the opened jacket.

The heady scent of a man and the warmth of the fabric make for an intoxicating mixture.

Justin sits beside me. He's close enough that I feel the heat of his body, yet far enough away that we aren't touching.

Bending my knees to my chest, I wrap my arms around my legs and look out at the pond. I turn to face Justin, taking in his profile as my stomach does flip-flops. "Have you ever worried that you'd ruin something if you say the wrong thing?" I ask.

He runs his palm over his face. "No. I'm usually the one to say the wrong thing without considering the consequences. It's a gift I have."

My cheeks rise as I smile, looking down and back up. "I'm not the type to slip away from a party." I reach out and lay my fingers on his arm. There's something electric in the touch. With his jacket off, the sleeves of his thermal shirt are pushed up and my fingers land on his muscular forearm. Quickly, I pull my hand away. "I don't mean to sound like I'm some crazy partier."

Justin is staring down at where I touched him.

Could he have felt the jolt I did, or is he upset we touched?

When his gaze meets mine, his lopsided smile grows. "I guess we can assess. You're not a crazy partier, and I'm not a creep or a perv."

"Can we?"

"Take my word for it."

"Are you to be trusted?" I ask with an unfamiliar flirtatiousness to my tone.

He lifts both of his hands as if in surrender. "The utmost trustworthy-est." He leans closer. "I can even keep the secret of your name."

"Well," I say, stretching out the word. "Back to this assessment of not being a creep or perv. Are you willing to answer a few questions?"

"Give it your best shot."

Turning toward him, I lift one eyebrow. "Have you ever walked around town in only a long raincoat?"

"Oh my God," he nearly shouts with a laugh. "That would be a hard no."

I lift both eyebrows. "Hard?"

That earns me a smirk.

"Okay, if we're doing this," Justin says, "and if I'm to believe you're not a crazy partier, you need to answer my questions."

"Seems fair."

"Have you ever awakened in an unfamiliar place, meaning you partied a bit too hard?"

"Never."

"Have you ever made what you later consider to be bad decisions based on the consumption of mind-altering substances?"

"How did you get a second question?" I ask. "I think it's my turn."

"Is that a yes?"

Shaking my head, I grin. "It's definitely a no. Now, have you ever stalked a girl, or guy if that's your choice, either in person or online?"

"Girl," he says definitively. "Woman, one of the female persuasion. I admit to a bit of social media stalking but never in person and only to...you know, get a better idea what she likes."

I scrunch my nose. "Hmm. That seems a little iffy."

"My intentions were pure."

"So, if I tell you my name, you'll search my online presence?"

"And if I tell you my last name, you won't?"

I shake my head. "No, Justin, I won't. I don't want to know what you post online. I'd rather get the answers to my questions by asking you, talking to you, you know... that old-fashion stuff."

The swirl in his blue eyes intensifies, like the sharpening of a camera's focus, staring directly at me.

"What?" I ask.

"I don't know. You're undeniably beautiful. Not a crazy partier and look young. Yet you're deep."

"Is that bad?"

"None of it is bad. It's a combination I'd like to get to know." He smiles a sexy grin. "In person. Not online."

His grin fades as the intensity of his stare grows. With each passing second, the pace of my heart rate picks up, my breaths come faster, and there's a twisting inside me like I've never known. His gaze moves to my lips, wordlessly pulling me to him as he leans toward me.

"That kiss?" he questions in a husky timbre.

Words fail me as I nod only seconds before his lips meet mine.

In that time and space, I'm too lost to realize I'm kissing Justin Sheers. Correction, I'm being kissed by Justin Sheers, kissed like I've never been kissed before. The energy radiates from him to me, a lightning bolt that sends detonations through my circulation. My skin heats from within. The longer it goes on, the slacker my body becomes.

I meld against him, hungry for his taste. It's desire, passionate and possessive with a hint of beer. I'm not certain when his hand came to the back of my neck, or when our faces turned, and moans escaped my lips. I don't even know when I fell back, my head on Justin's jacket as his tongue joins mine.

In twenty-two years, I never realized that a kiss could be so much. I'd read stories of fireworks and thought they were only that, fiction. As my breasts heave beneath Justin's strong chest, I am convinced, converted, a believer. My touch moves over his shoulders and to his head, raking my fingers through his hair as the sensation of his beard growth on my face and neck adds to my out-of-body experience.

Palming his scruffy cheeks, I pull back, panting for air.

Our noses were only millimeters away from one another.

"I think I got carried away," he says.

I'm not sure if it was meant as an apology, but none is necessary.

"I've never been kissed like that," I finally say. "I liked it."

"Me too." He sits up and offers me his hand.

I watch the way his fingers envelop mine. Everything about Justin is bigger than life. Sitting up, I readjust the large sweatshirt and look out to the pond. In the time since I slipped away from the party, the moon has risen above the trees, appearing smaller than it had yet no less bright.

"Do you see it?" he asks.

"What?"

"The man in the moon."

Smiling, I nod. "I do. I didn't when I was younger, and my brother helped me see him. It's not really a man but a face."

"Mystery woman has a brother."

Looking down, I sigh.

Jesus, Ricky would be furious at me and at Justin.

I start to stand.

Justin reaches for my hand. "I would like your number. No name if you don't want me to see your silly pictures on Instagram."

Together we stand as he reaches for his jacket.

"Who said I have silly pictures?"

"When did you graduate?" he asks, looking down at the sweatshirt. "From Purdue. I've been out for nearly ten years." He chuckles. "That sounds like college was prison. It wasn't."

Ten years.

Shit.

"This is a friend's shirt. I went to Ball State." *Go to Ball State. About ready to graduate.*

"What did you study?"

I take a step back, too afraid that he'll be able to connect the dots leading to my identity. "Justin, thank you." I look up, meeting his gaze. "I'm in a weird place. If things are meant to be, I'd love to see where this could go."

"I get weird places," he says, still holding my hand. "I think I'm in one too. I'm not much of a believer in fate. Giving me your number would be a better way of facilitating some unknown destiny."

A smile curls my lips. "And what would you put as my name in your phone?"

"Best kiss."

I drop my forehead to his chest, inhaling his scent. When I look up, I'm lost in the way he's looking at me. "Even with your name, I'd put that in my phone too."

"Are you ready to head back to the party?"

"I-I..." I reach for my phone and pretend to read a text. "Oh, it looks like my friends got bored. They're waiting for me just over that hill." There is a road that if I follow it far enough will lead to town.

"I can't let you walk by yourself."

"I'm a big girl, Justin."

"I'm not arguing. Let me walk you to the top of the hill."

"Just a minute." Turning away, I type out a quick message to Marilyn and Jill, telling them where to bring the car. After I hit send, I nod. "Okay."

Before we start walking, Justin reaches for my hand. For the first steps, we're silent, taking in the cool breeze while enjoying the warmth of each other's touch.

"Best Kiss," he says. "That's going to be your name until you tell me different. I think I'll shorten it to BK."

I giggle. "Okay."

He takes a deep breath and looks up to the sky. "I'm not...I don't want you to think...I'd like to see you." He laughs and stops, reaching for both of my hands. "As you can probably tell, I studied poetic muse at Purdue due to my mastery of language."

I laugh. "Education. That's my degree."

"Agriculture. I'm one of those people who want to do more than use the earth. I want to help it the way it helps us."

"Wow," I say genuinely. "That is poetic."

It's Justin's turn to laugh. "Not really."

In the distance, headlights become visible, going toward my rendezvous point. "I think that's my ride."

"BK," he says with a grin. "I won't give up."

"Stalker much?"

"You have no idea."

I push up on my tiptoes and brush his scruffy cheek with a kiss. "Thank you, Justin, for the best kiss of my life." I shrug. "All others pale. I'll hold your one kiss in my heart as the greatest." With that, I take off, walking before breaking into a jog as I make my way down to the street.

Chapter Six

Devan

My feet move faster and faster as gravity kicks in, increasing my speed as I run down the hill. One glance over my shoulder and I see that Justin is gone, no longer on the top of the ridge. Nearing Marilyn's car, I'm fighting to breathe, working to slow my steps in the soft ground, and despite the cool temperatures, I'm sweating like crazy under the big hoodie. My two friends are out of the car, waving their hands and screaming. I think they are. Mostly, I hear the sound of my circulation thumping in my ears.

Wait, they're coming at me. It's going to be a two-on-one attack and subconsciously, I know I'm about to fall to the damp grass. Consciously, I'm too freaked out to care. My feet slide as their voices come into range.

"Are you okay?"

"What happened?"

"Why did you disappear?"

"What was with the SOS text?"

As I stop like a runner coming into home base, I take another look over my shoulder to be sure he isn't watching. Suddenly, I'm on my behind, the sweatshirt and my jeans are covered in mud. My hysteria is on full display as I laugh so hard tears are coming down my cheeks.

Marilyn starts going on about friend code. "You tell someone. You know better…"

Still on the ground, I double over, breathing heavily, placing my hands on my thighs as I try to catch my breath.

"Oh my God, Devan," Jill says, "tell us why you sent the SOS code?"

Lifting one finger, I give them the universal *wait a second* sign and work to regulate the speeding rhythm of my heart. Standing up, I brush some of the mud and grass off my butt. Next, I pull the hoodie over my head, exposing my perspiration-saturated skin and camisole to the frigid night air. Goosebumps scatter across my skin as I lift my face to the stars, and a giant smile spreads across my face.

"Justin Sheers," I pant out.

The two girls look at one another.

"What about Justin Sheers?" Marilyn finally asks.

"I kissed him. No, he kissed me." I'm waving my hands. "Oh God, we kissed one another." As my words speed up, so does the twisting in my core and the tightening of my nipples—that could have to do with the cool temperatures. Nevertheless, my body is on fire.

Jill and Marilyn are now with me, holding onto my arms, their grips tightening. "What? *The* Justin Sheers?" Jill questions.

"Ricky's best friend," Marilyn adds.

Opening my eyes wide, I nod. "Yeah, that could be a problem."

"Wait," Jill says, shaking her head, "tell us every detail even if we'll be jealous."

"You're engaged," I remind her.

"Yeah, and I love Todd...but seriously...Justin Sheers is older, sexy, and all gruff and grumpy." Her eyes open wide. "Does he know how to kiss?"

OMG.

"Yes." My cheeks heat up. "Best kiss of my life."

"Did he know he was kissing Ricky's little sister?" Marilyn asks.

Pressing my lips together, I slowly shake my head.

"Oh, girl," they both scream.

I motion toward the car. "Let's get out of here. I don't want to be found out."

As the car doors slam and the sounds of nature disappear, I lay my head against the back seat and exhale. When I open my eyes, both of my friends are turned my direction.

"Details," Marilyn says.

I explain what happened by the pond, how he introduced himself—as if I didn't know him. And how

I never gave him my name; he called me BK. As I speak, I wonder again if I imagined the whole thing. Justin was sexy and sweet, not the boy who used to pick on me when I was young. As I tell the part about the intensity of his stare, my insides twist. Recalling his intoxicating scent, my nipples bead. Describing the sensation of his kiss, I know my panties are growing damp.

"I seriously didn't know people could kiss like that," I say with a sigh. "It was like the Fourth of July and Christmas morning all rolled into one."

Jill sits back against the window and pretends to fan herself. Marilyn's head is shaking.

"I thought you never liked Ricky's friends," my roommate says.

"I didn't like the way they picked on me. They always made me feel like a tagalong kid even when I was older." I think back and grin. "And honestly, I always thought Justin was kind of a...grumpy know-it-all."

"Apparently, he was hiding his secret sexy side from you," Jill says with one raised eyebrow.

"From all of us," Marilyn adds.

I sit taller, the small hairs on the back of my neck standing to attention as I turn my focus toward her. "You don't like him?"

"I obviously don't know him." She quickly changes her tone. "But, honey, if you're this excited, I'm happy for you."

"And a bit nervous," Jill says. "Seriously, Justin

wanted your name and number. I bet ten dollars he tells Ricky about the woman he met."

"BK," Marilyn says with a whimsical melody to her voice.

Jill's eyes widen. "Can you imagine when the pieces fall into place?"

The elation I was feeling only seconds earlier turns into something more akin to dread. "You're right." I inhale. "Let's leave Riverbend tonight. We can all go to Todd's place in Indy or back to Muncie. I'll call Mr. Sams tomorrow and tell him I'm a no for the job. It's official. I can never show my face in Riverbend again."

Jill laughs. "That's a bit drastic."

"Yeah," Marilyn says, "I'm glad Devan's not dramatic or anything."

The clock in the dashboard catches my attention. "It's just ten o'clock, and I made you both leave the party. I'm sorry I'm lame."

"Not lame," Marilyn says as she starts the car. "The hog roast was okay but not great. It was starting to break up anyway. I say we go to Bob's or Decoy Ducks."

Those are the two bars in Riverbend. Neither is as nice as big-city bars. They are more authentic as they probably have been for decades. Imagine wood paneling, neon signs with different beer slogans, pool tables, and of course, sticky floors. That said, they both are packed on the weekends.

"I'll go back to Marilyn's," I volunteer. "You two go out."

"Not happening," Jill says. "I have an idea."

After a stop at Marilyn's house to change out of my muddy jeans and get a new sweatshirt, and another stop at the liquor store—the only way to get cold seltzers in Indiana—we find ourselves back on the same dark road where we met an hour ago. "Is this crazy?" I ask with a giggle.

Our plan is to sneak back on the Gordon farm, climb into the hayloft, drink berry seltzers, and reminisce. The great thing about that hayloft is how there's an open area in the roof. We can watch the stars and stay warm, away from the cool breeze.

The party should be about over. It's past eleven, and too late for all the families with children. The older people will be home by now, watching the local news station. There may be a few stragglers. However, if we're quiet, we shouldn't be seen or heard.

The side of the barn facing the direction of the pond has a door that goes straight into the higher loft. From the other side of the barn, where all the festivities were, no one will ever see us.

"I'm more visible," I say as we climb the hill to the place where I left Justin.

"What do you mean?" Jill asks.

"My hoodie is red. Both of yours are black."

"Stay quiet," Marilyn scolds, "and no one will see us."

As we reach the precipice of the ridge between the pond and the Gordons' barn, we all stop. We're too far away to distinguish faces. Nevertheless, there are multiple figures standing near the simmering remains of the bonfire.

My mouth goes dry as I study each body shape. I'm no expert after only one kiss, but I'd bet my first paycheck that one of those people is Justin. The blood drains to my feet as I imagine another to be Ricky.

"Devan," Marilyn whispers as she slows and reaches for my elbow. "Are you all right?"

I shake my head. "I don't think this is a good idea." I jut my chin toward the fire below. "I'm pretty sure one of those people is Ricky, and if I'm right, there's a good chance another one is Justin."

"They won't see us," Jill says. "And maybe we can hear if they're talking about you."

About *me*.

"I'm going to be sick."

Jill reaches for my hand and tugs me forward. "No, you're not. Come on."

Reluctantly, I do as my friends bid and move toward the backside of the barn. We stay low to the ground, hiding in the shadows. If it wasn't for the gigantic knot forming in the pit of my stomach, this adventure would be fun.

My breathing catches as I realize why I'm afraid.

I don't want to be caught.

More than that, I don't want to be caught by Ricky and his friends and be made fun of, be made to feel like a child. That would be horrible. Even worse would be seeing the look on Justin's face when he recognizes me.

My mind conjures up the image of an angry Justin Sheers, one who is upset with me. I have no doubt that in my scenario, our one kiss would be a secret we'd both agree to take to the grave. That would also mean it would forever remain only one kiss.

Chapter Seven

Justin

"You boys are so sweet," Mrs. Gordon says with a smile.

Boys.

Everyone standing here is thirty years old or older.

That doesn't matter. Mrs. Gordon remembers when our parents were born. Her face is filled with wrinkles, and her hair is white as snow, and at the same time, she's as sweet as her kind ways.

"Thank you for making certain the fire is out," she says. "If you're sure you'll stay, I can go to bed."

"It's getting late," Ricky says.

"And cold," I say, seeing the heavy coat draped over her slumped shoulders. "We promise, Mrs. Gordon."

She reaches for my hand.

I look down, feeling the coolness of her touch.

"Bruce and I have been blessed to have all the men and women of Riverbend in our lives."

"I think it goes both ways," I say. "I can't imagine Riverbend without you or your farm." Yeah, maybe thoughts of the Dunn farm have me feeling sentimental.

Shaking her head, Mrs. Gordon's eyes grow moist as she speaks. "Your dad and his dad before him would help us back in the day, come by before we asked. Sheers boys have always been good ones and hard workers."

"Thank you, ma'am."

She turns to Ricky. "Same for the Dunn family. We're all staples of this land."

Ricky smiles and nods.

Mrs. Gordon moves around the fire, speaking to each one of us, telling a story about someone in our family. When she comes back to me, her smile is intact. "Good night, boys."

"Good night, Mrs. Gordon," we reply in unison.

"May I walk you to the house?" Harvey Russel asks.

"No." She waves him off. "The day I can't walk this farm is the day I sell." She pursed her lips. "And that's not happening anytime soon."

For a moment we stand silently and watch as the elderly woman makes her way toward her house. Without a doubt, Mrs. Gordon is a pillar of Riverbend. She and Bruce were friends with my grandparents. While the Gordons never had children, each generation has embraced them as family.

The five of us turn back toward the fire. To the side,

there are five-gallon buckets filled with water lined up, ready to douse the remaining flames. Everything else from the party has been cleaned up. The tables are down and most of the chairs are gone. We have a small ring of stadium chairs around the smoldering remains of the bonfire.

As people left, they took their dishes home. Even the large pig roaster is gone. The men who brought it here early this morning drove it back. One day, cooking the pig will be the responsibility of me and the men with me while the next generation will take care of the bonfire.

Before our group dwindled down to five, everyone worked together to gather the trash and put it in the back of Harvey's truck. Harvey is two years older than Ricky and me. His family owns the junkyard west of Washington. He'll take all the trash to the dump in the morning. The kegs are in the back of my truck. The tailgate is down, and there is still beer left to drink.

Nick Dancy finishes his beer and sighs. "I'll hang around here if any of you need to get home."

Two years younger than me, Nick was in Kandace's class. He owns a plumbing business in Washington. His parents moved to Tennessee a few years back. While he doesn't live in Riverbend anymore, he's one of our regular returns.

"I have no place to be," I say, flopping down in a stadium chair. While I'm looking at the glowing embers of the fire, my mind continually circles back to the woman near the pond. Each time it does, I feel my cheeks rise. It's crazy, but I'm almost afraid to talk about her.

Was she real?

I have nothing to show for our encounter.

No phone number.

No name.

And at the same time, with only one kiss, I feel different.

If I told Ricky my thoughts, he'd think I am either insane or drunk. Maybe both.

Truth is that the only beer I drank was before I went on that walk.

That could mean she was a hallucination, or that BK made me drunk in a whole different way. That kiss was unbelievable. I've heard that a first kiss should be special. In reality, I've had more than my share of uncomfortable first kisses. Those times when noses bump, we turn our faces this way and that, or the awkwardness that comes when one person is tentative and the other isn't. Just plain unpleasant.

Those are the times you tell yourself that it will get better. Let's be honest, it's because worse isn't really a way you want it to go. Nothing ever came of those relationships. If a kiss doesn't work, how could more?

In the hour or so since BK slipped away to her friend's car, I've tried to come up with something that was wrong about our encounter, some reason to forget what was the best kiss of my life.

I can't find one thing.

Thinking about her feisty dialogue, the way she dished it out and took it, her outward beauty, and the melody of her laugh all combined together makes me grin. Recalling the sweet taste of her lips has more of an effect on my mood than drinking ten beers. We shared a spark that I can't recall feeling before.

Ricky goes to my truck and fills two cups with beer and brings one to me. Handing it my way, he says, "Here. You seem...distracted."

Distracted.

I can't mention the sale of his farm in front of the other guys, so I simply shrug, put the cup on the ground by my chair, and looking over at Nick, I change the subject. "Who were you talking to tonight? That redhead."

"Jill Kohlberg."

"Oh," I say with my eyebrows raised. "Not ringing a bell, but she's not bad in the looking-good department."

Nick laughs as he stretches out his legs, moving his boots closer to the fire. He turns to Ricky. "You remember her, don't you?"

Ricky seems as dazed as the rest of us as he too stretches out his legs and peers up at the star-filled sky. "Yeah. I saw her tonight. She's one of the squealing girls who were always underfoot."

"Right," Nick says, "she hung out with Devan."

"Hmm." I try to recall the girls at Ricky's house. To be honest, I can't. They were nothing more than kids to me. And then I remember that Ricky said Devan is graduating from Ball State in another month. I turn to Nick. "Is there something maybe brewing between the two of you?"

He shakes his head. "She's too young for me. But more than that, the engagement ring on her finger is a big neon hell-no sign."

"Little Jill is getting married?" Ricky says with a hint of a question. "I wonder why Devan hasn't said anything."

"How often do you talk to your sister?" Harvey asks.

Ricky shrugs. "Once in a while." He laughs. "It's weird. She doesn't seem like a little kid anymore." He leans forward and lowers his voice. "At breakfast this morning, Cory told me he reached out to her to fill the seventh-grade science position at the middle school."

"No way," I say. "How can Devan be old enough to teach?"

"Weird how it happens," Ricky says. "I mean, I saw Jill. Almost didn't recognize her."

"Was Devan here?" Nick asks.

Pressing his lips together, Ricky shakes his head. "No. If she didn't cancel the interview with Cory, she probably came to town and left. Like I said before, Mom doesn't expect her to move back. I'm kind of shocked she even went to the interview. Hell, I meant to ask Cory how it went and forgot. Maybe she didn't."

"Who is Jill marrying?" Galvin, the fifth of our group, asks. Galvin is a year older than Ricky and me and lives in town—in Riverbend—but commutes to Bloomington where he is a chef at an upscale restaurant on Lake Monroe.

"Todd Blakely," Nick replies.

Everyone makes noises as I try to recall Todd Blakley, and then it hits me. "Wasn't he the one who shit his pants in elementary school? Even everyone at the high school was talking about how the whole bathroom stunk."

After we all laugh, Nick nods. "That was him."

Ricky grins my direction. "If I recall, Justin, you had to spray your pants with the hose because you didn't give it a shake, and you had an embarrassing wet mark."

I kick dirt his direction. "You swore to never mention that." Even though I act mad, I take everyone's laughs because Ricky is right. I was in that weird middle-school age and panicked. My plan worked. Only my closest friends knew what happened. "What's Todd Shit Pants up to these days?"

You would think we were a bunch of old ladies gossiping, not men in their thirties.

"Finishing up his MBA in Indy," Nick says. "Obviously, Jill has learned to overlook his childish mishap."

Galvin turns toward the large barn.

The structure is mammoth. I've helped fill it with straw and hay. I've also had a few happenings in the hayloft. I'd suspect over fifty percent of Riverbend at least made it to second base in that barn.

"Did you guys hear something?" Galvin asks.

I make another quick glance and turn away. "Creaky wood and wind."

"Or maybe someone is giving up their V card," Ricky says.

I scrunch my nose. "I'm not the voyeur type."

"It depends," Galvin says. "There's this one girl on pay-per-view…"

The conversation takes a drastic turn as Galvin and Nick expand upon the fetishes that keep their interest and those that turn their stomachs. I'm not listening. Instead, I'm back to the pond, to BK and me lying on my jacket, to the sounds of her moans.

Shit.

I stand, hoping no one notices my semi-erection. It sure as hell wasn't the talk of vibrators and anal fisting that made my circulation reroute. "I'm ready to douse this fire."

"Thank God," Ricky says.

Harvey agrees.

Each one of us lifts a bucket. The fire hisses and steams as the embers take on the water. I stack the buckets and carry them toward the barn. The heavy door creaks as I push it open. For a second, I think I hear something up in the loft. Standing still, I listen. My thoughts go to BK. I consider calling out but know it's stupid. She wouldn't be there.

Could she be with someone else?

Why does that upset me?

I don't hear anything else. The only sounds are those of the guys outside and the chirping of crickets. I take a moment and look out the large opening in the roof and see the stars.

With a sigh, I put the buckets in a supply room and make my way back out of the barn, closing the door behind me.

Ricky is waiting. He keeps his voice low. "Fuck, sometimes Galvin and Nick can get…" He doesn't finish the sentence. He doesn't need to.

I nod.

There are details of things I've done in private or in a hayloft—I think of BK—that never need to be shared. If I had a girl of my own, I'd be at home taking care of her, not droning on endlessly with friends about something I saw on the porn channel.

Chapter Eight

Devan

Five weeks later

"Devan Marie Dunn." My name echoes throughout Worthen Arena as I walk across the platform. The red and white tassel hanging from the mortarboard tickles my cheek as I reach for my diploma. It's an empty folder, but after the ceremony, it will be filled with proof of my degree.

I smile as a photographer takes my picture.

Stepping off the platform, I hear my brother's voice above the crowd.

"You did it, Devan."

Warmth fills my cheeks as I peer out at the audience. This is our last ceremony of the day. We started earlier this morning in the quad. The sun was shining, and the air was thick with excitement as we listened to prayers and speeches. Now, we're in Worthen Arena where both Marilyn and I receive our recognition.

Our parents are seated together along with Marilyn's older brother and younger sister and my brother, Ricky. Seeing my brother, I shake my head. He's standing and pumping his fist. I should be embarrassed, but I'm mostly proud—of graduating, of the gold cord around my neck signifying that I've graduated with honors, and of my family also being proud.

Ricky chose to attend a two-year college, earning his associate degree in bookkeeping.

I'm the first one to graduate with a bachelor's degree. My mom earned an associate from Indiana University in Indianapolis. She's been a dental hygienist in Washington all my life. My gaze meets hers, and I notice the tears in her eyes. It makes my heart swell to know they're proud of me.

After the ceremony, our two families dine at a local restaurant. The table is filled with Marilyn's parents, her siblings, and my family. Nine of us talking, laughing, and celebrating. Marilyn's mom, Joan, sits back and looks at me, a smile curling her lips. "I wish you could talk Marilyn into moving back. First, Marcus moves to Chicago and now Marilyn is moving away." She turns to her youngest daughter. "That's it, you can never leave."

We all laugh. Melissa is only fourteen. Her time is coming.

"I still can't believe it," Ricky says, talking to me. "I never pegged you for an RTS."

"I guess college doesn't count, so I'm not returning. I never left."

"College counts," Marilyn says. She turns to her mom. "And who knows what I'll do after grad school. Maybe I'll find a great kisser back in Riverbend."

I elbow my friend as my stomach does a flip-flop.

"What is this?" my dad asks.

"Nothing, Dad." My cheeks are on fire.

"You're moving back for some guy?" Ricky asks. "Who?"

"Like I'd tell you, if that guy existed."

My brother turns to Marilyn. "Does he?"

Marilyn shoots me an *I'm sorry* expression. "I'm just saying maybe I'll find a great kisser. And it isn't you," she adds. It seems there has been a rift of sorts between my brother and my best friend.

"Ouch," Ricky says, clutching his heart. "I'm so wounded."

"Have you two kissed?" I ask, shocked.

"No," they both say at the same time.

"And," Joan says, obviously moving the subject away from Ricky and Marilyn. Her eyes are on me. "You're going to live at home."

I move my gaze to my parents. They're both smiling, making me feel less like a failure for returning to my childhood bedroom. "I am for now. I want to see how the first year of teaching goes. Then maybe I can get an apartment."

"No rush," my mom says.

My parents were both enthusiastic about me taking the seventh-grade teaching position in Riverbend. They didn't blink an eye about me moving home. It was Ricky who let me in on the secret that they're considering selling our farm. He swore me to secrecy. It's the reason I'm laying the groundwork for moving out. I don't want my parents to feel trapped because I'm back in their house.

Later that night, Marilyn and I are back in our apartment for what will be our last night. We both sent a carload of things home with our families. Tomorrow, Dad, Art—Marilyn's dad—and Ricky are coming back with a moving truck.

"I'm going to miss living with you," I say.

"Me too. You can always move with me to Bloomington and commute."

I laugh. "I could live ten minutes from the school for free or live an hour away and pay rent."

"Yeah, but you get me."

"It would be worth it."

I go to the refrigerator and pull out a bottle of champagne that Joan left for us to toast our last night. Taking off the wire cage, I push up on the plastic cork. "Oh," I scream, jumping when the loud pop fills the air.

"We did it," I say as I lift a plastic cup with bubbly champagne and tap Marilyn's cup.

"We did."

We both take a drink. The bubbles tickle my nose and throat.

"Too bad all of our glassware is packed," she says, looking at the cup.

Peering around the mostly bare apartment, I think about all the things we've accumulated. "I'm glad you can use most of our stuff in your new apartment," I say. "I'd hate for it to be stuck in storage for a year."

"I appreciate it. I wasn't looking forward to buying new."

I pour more champagne into my friend's cup and, lifting one eyebrow, ask, "How come you never told me you kissed Ricky?"

She shakes her head. "Because it was a long time ago, and it only happened on a dare." She scrunches her nose. "No offense to your brother, but it wasn't the best kiss of my life."

A cold chill scurries over my skin. "Oh my God, you did kiss him."

"It was four years ago at your high school graduation party. And there were no fireworks. No butterflies. I mean, he's cute in a Riverbend type of way, but nope."

"Four years ago."

She nods.

"Does Jill know?"

Marilyn nods again.

"It's official. I need new best friends."

"What would you have said if you knew?"

"Eww. That would have been my first response." I recalled something. "Is that why you two don't get along?"

She shakes her head. "We get along when he isn't a dick."

"Is that why you weren't happy for me that night with Justin."

"I'm happy for you. I just know that it made things uncomfortable for me and Ricky. I don't want that for you and Justin."

Rolling my lip between my teeth, I think about the one kiss. Lifting my eyes, I meet Marilyn's gaze. "I don't know what it will be like when we see one another."

"Maybe you will fall into one another's arms and live happily ever after."

I laugh. "That's not where I'm placing my bet."

"What's your bet?"

"I'm leaning toward awkward silence."

Marilyn wraps her arm around my shoulder. "Someone is going to figure out what a wonderful catch you are. Who knows? It might be Justin Sheers."

That isn't a thought I can even consider.

"Just one kiss," I say.

I wake the next morning to the buzzing of my phone. Groggily, I lift the screen and squint at the light pouring in my bedroom window. With the drapes packed, the mini blinds don't do a great job of blocking the sunlight.

The text is from Dad.

· · ·

"ON OUR WAY. ART WAS CALLED INTO WORK. LUCKILY, RICKY TALKED JUSTIN SHEERS INTO HELPING. DO YOU REMEMBER HIM?"

Yeah, Dad. I definitely remember him.

He doesn't remember me.

My mouth goes dry as I look at the time of the text message. It was sent twenty minutes ago. That means I have about two and a half hours to come up with a disguise. Maybe a wig and a fake mustache.

Then I see a more recent text from my mom.

"YOUR ROOM IS DONE. I CAN'T WAIT FOR YOU TO SEE THE COLOR. I HAVE THE WINDOWS OPEN SO YOU CAN STILL SLEEP IN THERE TONIGHT."

That makes me laugh. When she told me she wanted to paint my room, I thought of what my best friends had said. It seems that we Dunns are nothing if not predictable. Well, not entirely. Throwing the blanket off me, I fling open my bedroom door, and rush across the hallway to Marilyn's room.

Bursting in, the door bounces off the wall.

"What's the emergency?" she mumbles.

"You have to help. I'm in so much trouble," I announce.

Rushing to my aid, Marilyn buries her face in her pillow.

Chapter Nine

Justin

Jack Dunn hands me a cup of coffee, lifting it to me in the back seat of his super-cab truck. The truck is about as old as mine, and in equally good shape. "Here you go." He meets my gaze. "Thanks again for helping us out."

I look back at the moving trailer we're pulling.

"What else could I be doing on a Sunday morning?" I say before taking the lid off the coffee. The steam and rich aroma swirl into the air.

"I bet Bridget would say church."

With a scoff I nod. "You're right, Mom would. And my dad would say there's work to be done."

Jack gets in the driver's seat and turns on the engine as we wait for Ricky to come out of the convenience store. "Rick told me you might be interested in our property?"

My stomach clenches. This is the first time Jack has talked directly to me about this subject. This conversation was a big part of why I accepted Ricky's request to help move his kid sister. Three hours each direction gives us ample opportunity to talk.

Clearing my throat, I say, "I hate to see it go to developers. I'd rather you keep it."

Jack's eyes meet me in the rearview mirror. "I'm getting too old for this work, just like your dad."

"You're younger than my dad. I get it. Dax" —my brother-in-law— "had an idea. Instead of selling, you could rent the land to us. I'll farm it. The ethanol is taking some of the guesswork out of the markets."

"Realtor said we should sell while the prices are good."

"Jack," I implore. Ricky and I have known one another our entire lives. We both call each other's parents by their first names. "It's fucking land. Barring a cataclysmic disaster, it's not going to depreciate. That developer wants to pay you pennies compared to what he'll sell it for when he chops it into little pieces."

We both turn to see Ricky walking across the parking lot with a box in one hand and a large cup of coffee in the other.

"We haven't signed anything." Ricky's dad nods. "Won't sign until we hear you out."

"What about Devan coming home? You don't plan to sell with her moving back in, do you?"

The side door opens as I finish my question.

"Do you what?" Ricky asks.

Jack smiles at Ricky. "Justin wants to know if Mom and I will kick you and Devan to the curb."

Ricky opens the box, filling the truck with the overwhelming scent of sugar. I swear I get a cavity simply by inhaling.

My friend shrugs. "I've been looking at a few apartments in town." He lifts a glazed cake donut, the one he knows I can't resist and hands it to me. "Here you go. I figure Devan can live with me if we have to."

"We're not selling the house out from under you," Jack says as he puts the truck in gear. "All this shit takes time. Devan moving home was unexpected but not a bad thing. It's making us take a closer look at our options."

With a mouth full of warm, sticky donut, I say, "I wonder why the developer hasn't come to talk to us."

"Said he did," Jack replied. "Your dad told him flat out he's not interested." His eyes meet mine again in the mirror. "As long as that land is your dream and Kandace and Dax are giving him grandbabies, Jack's not interested."

"So, I need to give you a grandkid?" Ricky says with a smile. "Give me nine months."

"Oh no," Jack replies with a laugh. His demeanor dims. "Rick, if it's your dream, speak up."

I look at my best friend, expecting him to say something. When he takes another bite of his jelly-filled donut, I shake my head. "What the fuck?"

Ricky turns to me. "I've been thinking back to when I was at Vincennes. I'm the one who keeps the books on the farm, and I'm considering going back to school, getting my bachelor's. Maybe I can have a real job, something with numbers. Maybe accounting. I can play farmer on the weekends and during harvest."

"Are you shitting me? How long have you felt this way?"

"It's been growing over the last few years."

"Why now?" I ask.

"Devan," Ricky says. "I'm proud of her."

She's a kid, I want to say.

"I'm not saying I want out of Riverbend," Ricky goes on. "I'm saying I might want to know there's money coming in without worrying about the weather."

His admission isn't a total shock. I've been hearing Ricky bitch about farming for years. I didn't realize that he was thinking of a way out. I force a smile. "My friend should follow his dream. Just remember, I can always use your help."

"I figured," he says as he stuffs another donut into his mouth.

Leaning my head against the window, I drift off. I wouldn't say I fall asleep. My mind fills with thoughts about the Dunn property. Dax was able to get some approximate numbers. The price of land has skyrocketed in the last few years. I admit to being shocked when he gave me an estimated value. Dad and I talked about buying, we have most of the capital, but damn, it would make things tight. Then Dax came up with the renting idea, and I was immediately on board.

As the truck bounces along 69 north toward Muncie, I can't tell if Jack took kindly to the idea of renting or if he wants to cut all ties. And then there are the thoughts of BK. It's funny how our mind builds things up—higher, better, bigger. I can't be certain if that's what I've done in the last month or longer...okay, five weeks last Friday since we kissed.

Who's keeping track?

Nevertheless, my memories of that one kiss have blown into much more than what happened. In my mind, I've taken our one kiss further. I've imagined her soft moans and tasted her sweet lips.

Five weeks.

BK said she wasn't currently from Riverbend.

Yet she was at the hog roast.

Pulling my hat over my eyes, I know I shouldn't spend my time thinking about some woman I'll probably never see again. Instead, I make an effort to return my thoughts to the Dunn property. I'm counting acres, calculating the price of seed...anything to avoid thinking about BK.

I've come to the conclusion that my mystery woman was only in Riverbend for one night with friends.

I'll never see her again.

I'm not being down on myself, simply a realist.

The one woman in forever to light a spark inside me will forever remain only one kiss.

BK.

"Justin."

Blinking my eyes, I hear my name on repeat. "What the...?" I push my cap off my face and blink, trying to focus as sunlight floods the inside of the cab. Shaking my head, I take in the surroundings. Jack Dunn is still driving. No longer are we on the interstate. We're driving through an apartment complex. All the buildings are three stories, and they all look exactly alike.

"You were snoring," Ricky says.

"Fuck you."

Jack laughs. "You were both snoring. So much for keeping me awake on the drive."

I think of something I should have thought of before as I look at the seat to my side. "Hey, are Devan and Marilyn both supposed to fit in this back seat?"

"No," Jack says, "They both have cars to drive back."

My focus goes to the building where we've stopped. I crane my neck toward the sky. "You didn't mention that she lived on the third floor. First floor? Right?"

"Oh shit." Ricky opens the door to the truck. "I forgot. She lives on the third floor."

Opening my door, I stuff the ends of my t-shirt into my jeans and turn my cap backward as I mentally size up a hundred trips up and down. "You're going to owe me more than donuts."

Jack presses a button outside the door. It makes a buzz sound.

"Jack?"

"Yeah, Marilyn," he says. "We're here."

"Okay," comes from the box. "Come on in."

There's another buzz.

"Tell me there's an elevator," I say.

Ricky bumps me with his shoulder. "I've seen you carry multiple bales of hay, railroad ties for fences, and more. Carrying a couch down three stories...you could do that alone."

"But I'm not."

We all laugh as we head up the stairs.

Each floor looks exactly the same. Same hallways. Same doors. The only difference is the numbers. I wonder how Devan and Marilyn could stand living in this box. This building—the entire complex—represents the shit I don't like. Give me a custom farmhouse, a wraparound porch, and land. I could never live in a box.

As we reach the third floor, there is a young woman standing in the hallway. From her dark hair, I know this is Devan's roommate. Honestly, I barely recall her as one of Devan's friends who used to follow us around.

She's grown up.

She's cute with a big smile. Her hair is in a ponytail, and she's wearing shorts with a Ball State t-shirt. "Come on in," she says. She lifts her arms and gives Jack a hug. "Thank you for helping. Sorry about Dad."

Jack pats her back and looks at Ricky and me. "Rick

brought his friend, Justin. Justin, this is Marilyn, Devan's roommate."

"Hi," I say, ready to get their shit down into the trailer and back home.

"Come in," she says. "We have everything ready to move."

"Is Devan here?" Jack asks.

"She is..."

Marilyn's voice fades away as my heart rate spikes and my gaze meets the soft brown eyes staring my direction.

No way.

This can't be real.

Her eyes shine as pink fills her cheeks.

"BK," I say too softly to be heard.

BK is Ricky's little sister.

Fuck.

She's Devan Dunn.

Chapter Ten

Devan

Justin's eyes widen as he scans from my hair to my shoes. With each passing second, the color drains from his cheeks. I want to talk, to say something, but my heart is beating too fast. I'm afraid if I try to speak, I'll pass out right here. The realization hits. I should have gone with the mustache and wig.

"I say we get the biggest things first," Ricky says, oblivious to the ringing in my ears or the tornado of thoughts swirling through my mind.

Justin's upset.

He's shocked.

He's mad.

He regrets kissing me.

He doesn't recognize me as the woman he kissed.

The kiss meant nothing to him.

Swallowing, I turn to my dad. "Thanks for coming all the way back up here."

Dad drops a kiss on my cheek. "Anything for you, baby girl. You know that."

Baby girl.

Great.

When I look back at Justin, he has his hat off, and he's running his fingers through his already-mussed auburn hair. His deep blue eyes are no longer on me. He's listening to Ricky's plan to empty our apartment as fast as they can.

The only person who sees what is happening is my best friend.

As tears threaten to break through my façade, Marilyn reaches for my elbow. "Devan, come with me for a minute."

Nodding my head too fast, I follow her back to her bedroom. She shuts the door and wraps her arms around me. It takes all my self-control not to cry. This is what happens when I let myself fantasize about a man and a kiss over the last five weeks.

"Are you all right?" she asks.

Swallowing again, I nod. "Yeah."

"This. This is why I was apprehensive that night." Her lips and nose scrunch. "Uncomfortable. I promise it gets better."

"Right. I don't know what I expected."

My best friend smiles. "Devan Dunn, I know exactly what you expected. You had a reunion in your mind where the world around you and Justin fades, music that only you two can hear comes into range, and despite your dad and brother standing right here, you and Justin are brought together by some magic magnetic pull until you're in his arms and your tongues are down each other's throat."

Hearing her say that scenario aloud makes me realize how far-fetched it was.

I playfully slap her shoulder. "No one's tongue is that long." I force a laugh. "And, smarty-pants, there wasn't music."

"Liar. I bet it was the song "Wings" and the Jonas Brothers suddenly appeared in our apartment."

"No," I say quickly. "It was Lady Gaga." I smirk. "Now, I'm thinking Miley Cyrus is best."

"Damn right. You can buy yourself flowers."

We turn at the knock on the bedroom door.

"Um, are you girls going to come out and direct traffic," my dad asks, "or are you giving Rick and Justin full control?"

Marilyn's and my gazes meet as we both start laughing.

Giving Justin Sheers full control is only a fantasy.

"We're coming," I call back.

"You good?" she asks in a whisper.

I nod my head. "I am now. Thanks, emotional breakdown avoided."

For the next two hours, the five of us work together. I admit to catching a glimpse of the way the muscles in

Justin's arms bulge when he lifts something heavy. I also notice that he doesn't shy away from big objects. Listening to Ricky and Justin argue as they take our couch down the two flights of stairs has us all laughing. It's like a bad recreation of an old *Friends* episode. We're lucky there are no holes in the walls to take away from our deposit.

We're all hot and dirty. The windows are open, and the warm spring breeze does little to cool the apartment. Yes, Marilyn and I are trying to save money by not using the air conditioning. Besides, the door is propped open.

Wiping my brow, I've pretty much decided that the kiss at the hog roast was completely a figment of my imagination. After all, Justin has barely spoken to me. Oh, he's said a few things such as...

"Is that box going in the trailer or in one of your cars?"

"How did you get this much shit?"

"What the hell is in this tote, barbells?"

You know, super romantic things but no admission that we kissed, well other than the way the blood drained from his face when he first walked through our doorway.

I'm in my bedroom, or what's left of it. The furniture is gone, and I'm double checking the contents of a tote when I hear the door close. Turning, my gaze meets the sexy blue eyes of my BK. Crouched down on the floor, I slowly make my way to my feet. Words aren't forming as my flesh heats and silence builds.

Justin removes his hat and wipes his brow with his

forearm. His t-shirt is stained with perspiration from all the work he's been doing and yet, as he takes a step toward me, I think he's the handsomest man to ever be alone with me in my bedroom. To be honest, he's the only man to be in this bedroom. My mouth goes dry as I try to read his expression.

"Are you mad?" I finally ask.

He snorts a response.

"I'm sorry," I say. "I guess you know why I didn't tell you my name."

"Yeah," he murmurs. His movements are short and jerky, walking one way and then another. His biceps flex beneath the hem of his short shirt sleeves and his boots sink into the carpet.

"Don't worry. I won't tell my brother."

"Fuck, Devan," he growls. "I know this can't go on." He stops mere inches away.

Warmth radiates off him in waves; despite his hard work, his scent is that of fresh deodorant and an intoxicating masculine aroma. Without more provocation, my body reacts to his proximity.

Shaking my head, I start to back away. "Don't worry about it. Nothing happened."

His hand comes to my chin, holding my jaw. Tightening his grip, he lifts it higher until we have eye contact. "Is that what you want?"

Unable to speak, I shake my head.

Justin's eyes are on my lips, staring at them as if he too is questioning whether our one kiss was real. My pulse speeds as my tongue darts out to my dry lips. In milliseconds, his lips crash down on mine.

Possessive.

Demanding.

Full.

Unlike the first kiss, this one is different. An exploratory mission to determine if the first kiss was real. By the way my nerve endings sizzle with electricity, my nipples bead, and my core twists, if I could speak, I'd say there's no doubt.

Justin tastes of coffee and sweetness.

His hand continues holding my face, controlling the way I turn and the way we move. His wide chest presses against my sensitive breasts. I've never been more turned on in my life. Lifting my hands to his chest, I feel the frantic rhythm of his heart as our kiss deepens.

I'm staggered by the realization that Justin knows who I am, and he's still kissing me. Not just kissing, claiming. I tell myself not to make too much out of this, but I'm not listening. When his lips part, without thought, mine do too.

It's as his tongue slides over mine that I let out a moan and press mine against his.

My fingers grasp the fabric of his shirt, twisting the material as my lips bruise. It's not all him. I'm pressing back with equal fervor. Hungry for—no, starved for— what I've only known with him.

Our bodies press together.

Mine melding with his as his hardens.

When Justin pulls back, I gasp, afraid he's regretting that he did it—that he kissed Ricky's little sister. Or worse, he is egging me on. This is some big prank, and he's about to laugh.

I'm ready to apologize again when Justin shakes his head.

"Fuck, Devan, I don't know what to do."

Letting go of his shirt, I take a step back, trying to ignore the erection trapped in his blue jeans. "It's okay," I say, "if you regret kissing me. Now and before."

His touch returns to my chin, gently lifting it. "Regret? Fuck no."

The sound of voices, Marilyn's, Dad's, and Ricky's can be heard coming from the living room.

"You don't regret it?" I ask softly.

"Do you?"

"No. But" —I jut my chin toward the door— "I don't know what to do about them."

"Right now," he says, wiping his hand over his handsome face, "nothing." His lips curl into a lopsided grin, and his blue orbs shimmer. "Maybe once you're settled, we can see each other?"

"Are you asking me out?"

"Unofficially."

No longer do I see my brother's cocky friend. Justin is adorable and sweet when he's uncertain. That is not the way he kisses. Heck no. There's certainty in his ability. It's this...talking...the unknown.

My confidence builds. "Let me know when it's official, Justin Sheers, and then I'll give you my answer."

As the door opens, Justin lifts one of the totes from the floor, holding it in front of him.

I contain my smile, knowing what he's hiding.

"There you are," Ricky says to Justin. "Why the fuck is the door closed?"

"Oh, was it?" I say as innocently as possible. Looking at the open window, I reason, "Probably the breeze."

Chapter Eleven

Justin

There are a thousand reasons why I shouldn't have kissed Devan again today. Two of them will be seated in the cab of the same truck for three hours later today. There is only one reason I can justify what I did—I wanted to. I wanted to know if I'd blown BK up in my memory, if she was not the absolute best kiss of my life. I thought that knowing her identity would take away from the way her touch affects me.

Part of me wanted it to be true, for the feeling to be gone.

It only took a second of my lips on hers, her face in my grasp, the sounds of her breaths in my ears to know I'd made a horrible mistake. I should have spent the day pretending I didn't recognize her. I should have kept with the mantra in my head about her being Ricky's little sister.

Newsflash—she isn't little anymore.

Shit.

I should have done almost anything other than kiss her again.

As soon as my lips captured hers, I was a fucking goner. I was already hard beneath my jeans before our tongues joined in on the action. Picking up that tote wasn't because it needed to be packed. It was my shield. The last thing I need is Ricky to notice I have a hard-on with Devan.

"Something wrong?" Ricky asks as we move things around in the trailer.

"Hangry."

"Yeah, me too. I'll take Devan's car and get us all some lunch."

"And leave me here to carry the rest of the shit down?" I shake my head. "Let's find out what everyone wants, and I'll go get it." Yes, and I consider staying away until the trailer is filled. Staying away from the little firecracker upstairs that makes me want to forget everything and everyone but her.

Jack appears at the opening of the trailer with a large tote in his hands. "I'm running to McDonald's. Can I get you two something?"

Shit.

There goes my chance at a reprieve.

We give Mr. Dunn our orders and head back up the

stairs toward the apartment. Once inside, I stay out in the living room, making damn sure not to go back to Devan's bedroom again. Taking a moment, I turn a full circle, curious what this place looked like before it was all boxed up.

"Justin," Ricky calls, "get your ass in Marilyn's room."

I walk down the hallway, purposely not looking in the other bedroom.

"Fuck," I mumble, seeing the tall dresser. "How did we miss that?"

"It was in the closet," Marilyn says with a grin. "Sorry."

Gritting my teeth, we remove the drawers, still filled with clothes. After Ricky and I carry the shell of the dresser down to the parking lot, we start shifting shit around inside the trailer to make room. Marilyn and Devan make two trips apiece carrying the drawers. We finally have it all settled when Jack drives up with our food.

"Our table is in the truck," Marilyn says, tilting her head. "There's a picnic table this way." She takes the tray of large drinks and walks between two buildings.

Saying I'd rather eat alone is on the tip of my tongue, but then I see Devan turn the corner, headed back upstairs. Walking with Jack and Ricky, the three of us carry the food and follow Marilyn. I stop, taking in the scene. On the other side of the cookie-cutter box buildings is a pond, manicured grass, and trees. The picnic table is beneath the shade of a flowering tree. As I sit and unwrap my burger, I wonder where Devan went. As time passes, I wait for someone to bring her up. No one does.

Jack and Marilyn are laughing and talking about when the two girls moved into their freshman dorm room. Ricky is busy making sure he gets every French fry from the container. Taking a bite of my sandwich, I wait. This isn't like me. I'm hungry, hangry even, yet why isn't Devan down here eating? She must be hungry too.

I notice the box of nuggets and large fries sitting untouched, getting cold.

I can't take it any longer. "Where is Devan?"

Ricky looks around as if he didn't notice she was missing. Seeing as he's on his second quarter pounder, he might not have noticed.

"I'll go check on her," Marilyn says.

Tossing my burger onto the open wrapper, I stand. "I'll go."

As I'm making my way back into the building, my mind starts with all kinds of crazy scenarios. We've left the damn door to their apartment open all morning. Maybe someone was in there when she got there. Their mission was to rob her, but she doesn't have anything left up there. The thieves got angry. My thoughts go darker.

I'm running by the time I get to the second staircase and clenching my jaw so hard my teeth ache. Breathing heavily, I get to their apartment. The door is closed.

Fuck.

I reach for the handle, but it's locked.

Someone has her inside.

What if she's unconscious?

What if they've hurt her?

Making a fist, I pound on the door. "Devan, open up. Devan." I call her name. I'm about to kick the damn door down when it opens from the inside.

Her smile is breathtaking. "Whoa, what's the emergency?"

Standing tall, I look over her shoulder into the apartment. My heart is beating so fast, I'm surprised she can't see it through my shirt. "Um, are you okay?"

"Yeah," she says with a grin as she lifts a jar of mayo. "I had to dig in the cooler. I love dipping my fries in mayo."

"That's disgusting."

"Have you tried it?"

"No," I admit.

"Then don't knock it." She steps into the hallway and closes the door.

I stuff my hands into the pockets of my jeans, afraid if I don't, I might reach out and touch her, hold her hand, or do something I shouldn't. Looking at the door, I ask, "Is it locked?"

"What will anyone take?"

"It's better to be safe."

She reaches for the handle. It rattles rather than turns. "Locked."

The tension eases from me as we turn toward the staircase ready to join the others for lunch. I contemplate explaining why I was banging on her door like a wild man, but I'm not confident that an explanation will help things. Instead, I ask, "What made you decide to move back to Riverbend?"

"Are you really gone if it's only for school? You went to Purdue, right?"

"Yeah. I never imagined staying away."

"I did," she says wistfully. She turns, her light brown eyes full of wonder. "If I told you, you'd probably go back to thinking of me as only a kid."

My cheeks rise as I grin. "I'm not thinking of you as a kid. My little problem earlier wouldn't have happened if I thought you were a kid."

"Little?"

That makes me laugh. "A discussion for another time. Your move back to Riverbend?"

We're now outside and as Devan lifts her face to the breeze, the sun hits her like a spotlight. The color of her eyes reminds me of soft suede. Browns and golds blend in the most unique of ways. Her hair is light yellow, and in the sunlight I see darker shades in it.

"I think I wanted the adventure of leaving, but when it came down to living, I wanted the familiarity of Riverbend."

I lower my voice as we are closer to the others. "I was hoping it was that best kiss."

Pink fills her cheeks as she looks at me and away.

"I found her," I say as I take my seat at the picnic table.

Devan sits on the other side beside Marilyn and opens the jar of mayonnaise.

"Your food is cold," Ricky says to her. "I was about to eat it for you."

Devan dips a fry right into the jar.

Lifting my sandwich to my lips, I try to hide my smile. Watching her place each fry between her plump lips is the sexiest thing I've seen. And despite the mayo, I don't find it the least bit disgusting.

It's nearly three in the afternoon when we close the trailer and secure the door. Nothing is left in the apartment, and both the ladies' cars are filled to the brim. I'm even sharing the back seat of the truck with a laundry basket filled with blankets, and on the floorboard are three potted plants. My task is to make sure they stay upright.

Jack waits for Devan and Marilyn to pull out before he follows them. My first thought is that the ride back will take twice as long. With my mom and sister as the measurement, my experience is that women drive much slower than men. However, once we're on the interstate, I take that thought back. Pulling the trailer slows us down. Devan and Marilyn leave us in their dust.

"Thanks again," Ricky says as he cranks up the air conditioning.

"Third floor," I say. "You owe me." The unstated truth is that I'm glad I came. The mystery of BK is solved. Now the question is what to do with the knowledge. This morning's kiss comes to mind.

"I told you," Ricky says, bringing me to the present.

"Told me what?"

"She's not a little kid anymore. It's like she left for Ball State and suddenly is an adult."

"You're all kids," Jack says.

All I do is nod. There's really not an answer that I can give, one that won't either get me punched by my best friend or tossed from his dad's truck.

Chapter Twelve

Devan

I wait until we're on the interstate before I hit the call button on my steering wheel. Marilyn's name is at the top of the recent calls list. Before I can give the car instructions to connect a call with Marilyn James, my car fills with the melody of an incoming call. Marilyn's name is on the screen.

"Answer call," I tell my car.

"I can't believe you haven't called me. Oh my God, what happened in your bedroom? I started to freak out when I saw the door closed. You could see the mental math happening with your dad and brother. That's why I got all loud. What did we interrupt? It's killing me. Why haven't you spilled?" Her questions come too fast for me to answer.

Gripping the steering wheel, I laugh.

"You're not talking."

"You haven't given me a chance," I say between giggles.

"I mean, it was obvious that after...you were happier. Did he say something? Do something? What happened?"

Hitting my cruise control, I lean back against the seat. While I'm watching the traffic around me, my thoughts go back to late morning.

"Devan, if you don't talk, I'm unfriending you."

"You wouldn't do that," I say.

"You're right. So talk."

"He kissed me again." I pause a second. "A real kiss."

The sound of Marilyn's shriek fills my car.

The ear-piercing squeal is loud enough for me to look in all my mirrors to be certain there isn't a siren behind me.

"Was it...? Was it as good as the night of the hog roast?" my best friend asks.

"Better."

"Oh, you need to call Jill. She won't believe it. Did he say anything? Did you?"

"I told him it was okay if he regretted either kiss or both kisses now that he knows who I am." I sigh. "He said he didn't. He asked if I did."

"And you said no."

Nodding, my smile grows. "He said once I'm settled, maybe we could see each other."

Marilyn's volume rises. "He wants to go on a date?"

"He said unofficially."

"And you said…?"

A smile blossoms on my lips. "I told him to ask me when it can be official."

"You didn't."

"I did. I mean, sneaking could be fun, but I don't want to end up as a notch on Justin Sheers's belt, and then forever be connected to him through Ricky."

"Damn," she says, elongating the word. "That's a tricky tightrope."

Sighing, I nod. "I know. I mean, even if we date officially, if things don't work out—"

"Stop," Marilyn demands, interrupting my thoughts. "Don't speak negative energy into this. Think positive. I mean, if I would have been asked what would happen once he learned who you are, kissing you again wouldn't have been in my top five answers. He did. You did. Oh, did you kiss again when he went to find you for lunch?"

"No," I say with a smirk, recalling the way he was banging on the door. "He was a little frantic when the door was locked, but on the way to the picnic table, we just talked. He asked why I wanted to move back to Riverbend."

"Did you tell him it was his kiss?"

"That's not the only reason. And no, I didn't tell him that. I told him that I like the familiarity of Riverbend."

"Yeah, don't give Justin Sheers a bigger head than he already has. Oh, my mom is calling," Marilyn says. "I'll call back when I can. Drive safely."

"You too," I reply before the call drops. I'm thinking about her last statement.

Does Justin have a big head? Meaning, is he conceited?

I might think he is if I hadn't heard the uncertain tone in his voice as he asked about maybe seeing one another. When I think back on him when I was young, I guess I thought he was a grumpy know-it-all. Now I'm seeing him in a different light. Justin knows what he knows. From what I've heard Ricky and Dad say, Justin is the reason the Sheers farm is productive. His research with alternative uses for corn has helped others in the area as well as his family.

Personally, I think it's great that he's carried on the tradition of farming. I'm pretty sure Ricky is tired of it. And with the news that Mom and Dad are considering selling the property, it seems as if the Dunn farm will go the way of other farms. The idea of it being broken into small pieces with tiny lots and big houses makes my stomach turn.

Thinking about that, I wonder if I will stay in Riverbend. I mean, it won't be the same if it all changes.

As I pull off the street onto the lane that leads to our house, my childhood home where I will now again live, the sun is near the horizon, the sky filling with vibrant shades of crimson. The big white barn is the first thing you see. There are still pens where we used to have livestock. When I was a kid, there were cows and goats. When our dad was young, they raised pigs. Now we've gone to concentrating on agriculture—growing corn, soybeans, and hay. Cultivating straw.

Maybe there's no stopping changes.

They happen whether we want them to or not.

As I'm getting out of my car, the screen door flies open, and Mom comes out on the porch. Even though I saw her yesterday, she's coming toward me with a smile as if it's been months. Her arms open wide as she pulls me to her. She's a little bit shorter than I am with the same light color hair. Hers is cut into a cute short style. In her mid-fifties, she's still in great shape.

"I'm so glad you're home," she says.

"What color is my room?"

Her smile grows, making small lines near the corners of her eyes. "I hope you like it." She looks at my car. The entire inside, minus the driver's seat, is filled with stuff. "I'll help you carry some things."

"First, I want to see my room." I know that since I asked to come home, my mom has been excited about redecorating my room. And by her palpable excitement, my answer is exactly what she wants to hear.

Together we go up the steps of the porch. It's one that wraps around two sides of the house. There's no rail, only columns every ten feet or so. On each side of every column, Mom has flowerpots with bright red geraniums. And in the middle of each set of columns is a hanging fern. While most people buy their flowers from a local nursery or a big-box store in Washington, Mom raises hers in a small greenhouse Dad built for her on the backside of the big barn. The greenhouse windows face south, giving it all the warmth needed in the winter months so that in the spring, they're ready.

I look at the flower beds near the porch. "You haven't planted the beds yet."

"I've been painting. Maybe you can help me with the flower beds."

Nodding, I grin. "I'd like that."

Our house was built by my dad's grandfather. It's had a lot of renovations since then, such as plumbing. Grandpa used to tell stories about an outhouse. As we enter the kitchen, the air is filled with a glorious aroma. On the stovetop is a large stockpot. "Chili?"

"I figured you'd all be hungry after packing all day." Mom goes to the stove and removes the lid. The scent of chili powder wafts around the room. Stirring the chili, she says, "I told Rick to invite Justin. It was so nice of him to help."

My circulation slows, falling to my feet and leaving me faint. I reach for the back of one of the kitchen chairs and hold tight. "Is he coming?"

"Justin? I don't know. I made plenty." She taps the large spoon on the edge of the pot, puts the lid back on, and lowers the flame beneath the burner. "Are you ready?"

For Justin to be at my house.

No.

Mom's smile grows. "Let's go see your room."

"For my room," I say softly, "I'm definitely ready."

The back staircase steps creak as we go upward. There wasn't much uniqueness that went into planning homes back in the day. At the top of the stairs there's a landing and a hallway with five doors. At the far end is another staircase leading to our front living room.

Four of the doors access bedrooms and the fifth is to a bathroom. When plumbing was installed, a wall was taken down and a small bathroom was added in what is now Mom and Dad's room. The renovation made their bedroom larger than the rest. The other three rooms are all about the same size. Ricky had his own bathroom until I came along.

Mom opens the door to my room. Her brown eyes, the color of my own, are on me. The lavender walls I've had for as long as I can remember are gone, now painted a pale peach color. One wall, the one with the windows, is a few shades darker. The tall windows have light, wispy white drapes over plantation style blinds. The woodwork is painted a shiny white, a great contrast to the darker wall.

"I love it," I say, giving Mom a hug.

"I have another surprise."

"Another?" I follow her into the hallway and down to the last room on the right.

When she opens the door, I see the same colors as my bedroom. "Where is your craft table and supplies?"

"I figured a teacher, especially a first-year teacher, will need someplace to work when she's not at school."

"Mom, you didn't need to give up your room."

She's shaking her head. "My eyes aren't good enough for cross-stitch, and my days of scrapbooking are done. Mostly, this room had become a catchall. You gave me a reason to clean it all out."

A smile breaks out over my lips. "Thank you. I will definitely help you plant flowers."

The sound of Dad's truck can be heard through the open windows.

"If Justin is here," Mom says, "he can help Ricky bring your desk up to your office."

My office.

That thought fades with the realization that I need a shower. And then I remember how hard Dad, Ricky, and Justin worked. We all need showers.

"Mom, they worked all day. My desk can wait." Out the window of my new home office, I see Dad pull his truck in, the trailer in tow. From high above, I can watch without being seen. Ricky gets out of the passenger side. It takes a minute, but Dad is the next to get out. They're both walking toward the house.

Mom is peering over my shoulder. "Oh, it looks like Justin couldn't make it."

I shouldn't be disappointed, but I am.

Spinning, I meet my mom's gaze. "Do you mind if I take a quick shower before dinner?"

"You go ahead."

I brush her cheek with a kiss. "Thank you for both rooms. I love the colors."

Mom's eyes light up. "I'm glad you're home."

Chapter Thirteen

Justin

Banging the heel of my hand on the steering wheel, I ask myself for the hundredth time why I couldn't have said no. I could have. I should have. I didn't.

Jack Dunn took me home. He'd picked me up early in the morning so Dad would have my truck if he needed it. I should have said good night. Instead, when he said Janet, Ricky's mom, made chili and would like to have me over for dinner, the word yes came out of my mouth. I wasn't exactly sure where it came from. I recognized my own voice, but damn. I'd just spent the entire day with the Dunns. A shower and relaxing at home would be the usual end to my day. There is probably even a baseball game on. If the Cardinals are playing, Dad and I could sit and yell at the umpires all night.

Instead, I gave my mom a thirty-second explanation on why I was eating with Ricky, ran upstairs and stripped out of my sweaty clothes, took a fast shower, and here I am, driving back to the Dunns' farm with wet hair, fresh clothes, and feeling like a teenager, not a thirty-two-year-old man.

I slow my truck as I'm rounding a bend. In the stream of my headlights, I see the overgrown brush. The white petals of wild daisies catch my eye. For a moment in time, I consider stopping, picking a bouquet for Devan.

As soon as the thought comes, I dismiss it. Looking up at the growing dark sky, I shake my head. "Therapy. Intervention. Shit, I need something."

The response to my own statement comes to me.

"I'm talking to myself," I say aloud. "It's official. I'm losing it." I slam on the brakes and pull off to the side of the road. The Dunn farm is only two miles away. On these dark roads, I could be there in less than five minutes. Glancing to my right, I see my phone in its holder. Picking it up, I type out a text.

"SORRY, RICKY. THERE'S SHIT TO DO HERE. TELL YOUR MOM THANKS. I'LL TAKE A RAIN CHECK."

I scrunch my nose. Rain check

Who the fuck says rain check?

Backspacing over the last sentence, I try again.

"…MAYBE ANOTHER TIME."

Do I want another time?

Is that too forward?

Will Ricky think it's weird?

Back space again. The cursor sits after the word 'thanks.' Yeah, that will do. I don't need any more explanation than that.

"Fuck," I growl as I throw my head back.

Swallowing, I remind myself I've eaten hundreds of meals at the Dunns' house. Ricky has eaten hundreds at my house. Never once in the past have I been a pussy about it.

Pussy.

My breathing quickens.

Oh, dear Jesus, don't go there.

At least my self-talk is no longer audible.

Without sending the text, I throw the truck into drive. Gravel pelts the bottom of my truck as I head toward the Dunns' farm. Nothing has changed as I pass the big white barn. The lane is dark with only the illumination of my headlights until I turn and make my way toward the garages. The old house is lit up. Parking my truck next to Devan's car, I see that it's still filled with shit. The trailer probably is too. No time to unpack since they made it home.

My palms are sweaty as I push my hands into my jean pockets. A floodlight comes on as I walk toward the house. By the time I knock, my mouth is dry.

Janet Dunn calls from inside. "Justin, come on in. Family doesn't knock." She's placing bowls on the table filled with chili toppings. There's cheese, sour cream, onions, and crackers. Ricky's mom—Devan's mom—smiles at me. "I'm glad you could make it."

"Um, Jack said..." I shrug. "Thanks for inviting me."

"What can I get you to drink? Everyone is upstairs cleaning up. It sounds like you had a busy day. I'm so glad you could help. Jack thinks he can carry a couch, but he can't. You probably saved him from traction." She laughs.

"Iced tea," I say, rocking back on my heels and looking around. The large kitchen is the same as it was before I knew BK's identity, and yet it feels totally different.

"We have some craft beer from that new brewery in Bloomington," Ricky says as he enters the kitchen. His dark blond hair is wet, and he's pulling a clean shirt over his bare chest.

My thought isn't about the beer, but that, hopefully, my showering won't be seen as odd. It isn't like I'm trying to impress...it's a shower. Ricky showered too.

Devan comes down the back staircase, typing on her phone with a big smile. It's when she looks up that her smile momentarily disappears. "Oh, Justin. I thought you couldn't make it."

"Devan," Janet says, "where are your shorts?"

Devan lifts the hem of the sweatshirt, revealing sexy, soft short-shorts.

"Most of my clothes are still packed," she says. "I found these in my dresser."

"We have company…"

"I don't mind," I say.

Ricky's sister.

Little Devan Dunn.

The internal monologue isn't working.

Devan smiles my direction and turns to her mom. "See, no complaints."

And then I remember that Devan said she thought I couldn't be here. Did someone tell her that? I turn to Janet. "If you weren't planning on me…"

"Nonsense. We have plenty. I was counting on you." Before I can respond, she calls loudly for Jack.

Once he's with us, everyone fills their bowl and takes seats around the table. Before sitting, Ricky goes out to the garage refrigerator and comes back in with a large growler. I'm seated across from Janet, Devan is at her side, and Jack and Ricky are at each end. Ricky pours dark beer into glasses for me, Jack, and himself.

"Hey," Devan says, "I'm old enough to drink."

Old enough.

What does that mean?

I try to do math, to remember exactly how much

younger she is than us. She just graduated college. That makes her twenty-two. I think. I'm thirty-two. I've never felt old before now. As I'm trying to figure out the dilemma, Devan and Ricky are sparring.

"Seriously?" Ricky asks his sister. "This is beer."

"I know that. I drink beer."

He looks to his mom who nods, before reaching for another glass. "Mom? Do you want some too? I don't want to leave you out."

"I'll pass," she says with a smile. "Everyone help yourselves to any toppings. Jack also has his special hot sauce if my chili isn't hot enough for you."

In the past, I've made the mistake of trying Jack's hot sauce. It's a homemade concoction from peppers the Dunns grow in their garden, and it's deadly—like straight from Hell. Seriously, Jack should sell it to the government. One bottle could take out an entire cartel.

Ricky shakes a few drops of hot sauce in his bowl and hands the bottle to me. Instead of adding the fiery liquid, I put the bottle on the table and dip my spoon into the red soup. While the chili is hot, as in temperature, evidenced by my melting cheese—the flavoring is perfect. "Very good," I murmur. "Plenty hot."

Devan hides her smile as she too leaves the bottle of hellfire untouched.

I suddenly wonder if consuming Jack's recipes would be necessary—a hazing of sorts—to enter the Dunn family.

Would I do it?

Wait. No, I'm not thinking of that.

Despite my inner turmoil, the conversation around the table stays mostly lighthearted as Devan and Ricky recount the day's activities.

My bowl is almost empty when Ricky's story registers.

"...couldn't find Justin. And he was in Devan's *bedroom*." He accents the word. "Door was shut."

Coughing, I choke on the chili as my eyes meet Devan's. Sitting taller, she shakes her head. "Jeez." She looks at her mom. "We had the windows open, and with the front door also open, other doors kept slamming."

Ricky laughs as he points his spoon at me. "Man, you should see your face. I was just razzing. Seriously, thanks for the help today."

"Speaking of help," Janet says, "Justin, before you leave, could you help Rick get a desk from that trailer up to Devan's new office?"

"Devan has an office?" Ricky asks.

"I never use that craft room."

"Why does she get an office? I do the books for the farm."

"And you use the office on the first floor to do that."

"But that's Dad's office."

As Janet and Ricky go back and forth, I steal a glance across the table. Devan's hair is still damp, making it appear darker than before. It's piled on her head with cute bouncy curls around her ears. Her face is freshly washed and without makeup. And while I can't currently see them, I have absolutely no complaints about the length of her shorts.

While Devan's trying not to look up, she's stunningly beautiful in a real and genuine way.

I've never been a big admirer of made-up women. In my mind, the amount of makeup worn has a negative correlation to their beauty. It's not that those women on TikTok and Instagram are unattractive. I simply find natural much more appealing.

"May I get you some more chili?" Janet asks.

"I'm good," I reply.

"Oh, surely you worked up more of an appetite than that."

"I did," Devan says, walking to the stove. Bending forward, she takes a second helping.

A smile curls my lips. I'm loving the shorts. It's also because of Devan's appetite. Today for lunch, she ate all her chicken nuggets and the entire large order of fries with mayo—gross. Now, she's getting herself a second helping of chili. I can't help thinking about times when I've taken a girl out on a date and she barely picks at a salad, as if eating in front of a guy is a crime.

Truth is, I would like more chili.

"I think I will have seconds," I say, pushing back the chair. "I can get it myself."

Devan sets her bowl on the table and reaches for mine.

As our gazes meet, it's one of those surreal moments. "Really," I say. "I'm capable."

"I'm sure you are," she says, taking my bowl from my grasp. "I'm up already." She carries my bowl to the stove, the hem of the sweatshirt covering all but an inch of her shorts—not that I'm looking. When she brings the filled bowl back, I catch the scent of flowers. It's not overpowering, simply the perfect, sweet aroma.

After dinner, Ricky, Jack, and I go out to the trailer as Janet and Devan clean up the kitchen.

Of course, the desk Mrs. Dunn wants us to carry upstairs isn't packed near the opening to the trailer. Getting to the massive piece of furniture takes time, removing totes, boxes, and other furniture. We pile everything in the garage until we reach the desk. Getting the couch down the stairs in Muncie was a piece of cake compared to getting this long desk upstairs with turning corners.

We start using the back stairs, but the narrow stairwell makes it impossible. The front staircase is open and works better. Then there is the negotiating around corners. By the time we succeed, my fresh shirt is damp from perspiration. Back in the kitchen, I say good night. For a moment, I consider asking Devan to come out to the car with me.

Instead, I stuff my hands back in my pockets and head toward my truck.

Chapter Fourteen

Devan

"I'm going to go get a few things from my car," I announce to my family who all seem disinterested. I peek over my shoulder to see if I'm being watched before I head toward the door, following Justin. As I debate calling to him, the screen door behind me slams, and he turns. My steps slow as he grins in the moonlight.

The floodlight near the garage comes on, bathing us both in bright illumination. And in that moment, I worry that I am being too forward. Maybe I should have stayed indoors.

Without a word, Justin steps from the bubble of light into the shadows at the end of the garage. Before he disappears, I see him tip his head for me to follow. I take one last look back at the house. The kitchen windows are open to the spring breeze. They're filled with a golden light, yet no one remains in the room. They've moved on. If I were to guess, Dad is in the living room. Mom is in her room, and Ricky is either with Dad or in his room. Or he could still be complaining to Mom for giving me the extra room.

I walk carefully, the gravel sharp under my bare feet. I'm watching the ground, careful where I step as I slip behind the far end of the garage and run face-first into a brick wall. Strong hands reach out to steady me as I bounce backward.

Justin's solid grasp of my arms keeps me from falling. I crane my neck upward until I see his eyes. In the kitchen I was noticing how blue they are. A deep cobalt reminding me of the summer sky. Now, they appear black, his pupils dilated in the darkness as his stare goes to my lips.

"I want to kiss you again," he says, his deep voice rumbling through me.

"I won't stop you."

He turns us. In less than a second, my shoulders are against the garage. Justin's hands are on either side of my face, and his solid body is in front of me. His masculine scent fills my senses as his gaze rakes over me.

Without a word, he takes my chin in his grasp.

Gentler than this morning, Justin moves slowly and deliberately, taking his time.

Butterfly kisses and nips pepper my lips, warming me from the inside. As my breathing hitches, his kisses become deeper. His lips take mine—consuming me. Justin's actions are as if he's starved for our connection.

His hunger is contagious.

I feel him everywhere. While it's only a kiss, every cell within my body sparks to life, flickers igniting into flames. When his tongue seeks entrance, I willingly part my lips. It's as his kisses leave my lips, moving to my neck, the sensitive skin behind my ear, and onto my collarbone that my fingers weave through his hair, and I push my hips toward his hard frame.

Justin sighs as he pulls back. With one hand on the wall, his other is caressing my arm. "How did you learn to kiss like that?" he asks, his lips quirking into a grin.

My pulse is too fast, and my nipples too hard.

Licking my lips, I grin. "I've never kissed like that before."

"I don't believe you."

Reaching for his shirt, I lay my hand on his chest. "I'm always honest. It's okay if you think I need more practice."

His grin grows. "I think you've perfected the task, but I'm willing to help you out if you're looking for a practice partner."

"I am," I say, pushing up on my tiptoes and meeting his lips with mine.

Justin spreads his legs, straddling mine. With his hands on my hips, he moves them higher, under my sweatshirt. My flesh is ultrasensitive to his touch. If he moves a few more inches, he'll learn that I'm not wearing a bra.

However, his hands don't move higher. His fingers splay on my lower back as his touch hovers in safe territory.

Safe isn't the right word.

Having his hands on me, beneath my shirt is a whole new experience. I'm ultra-conscious of his touch. The coarseness of his fingers is like flint striking against steel. The temperature within me rises, yet he takes each step slow, not pushing me.

When he backs up, he grins. "For the record, I like your shorts."

My cheeks grow warm. "I didn't know you would be at dinner. I saw Dad and Ricky get out of the truck and assumed you didn't want to be here."

"I almost turned around."

"Why?"

"Because, BK, you have me not thinking straight. On the way here, I almost stopped and picked daisies."

I laugh. "I like daisies."

His forehead drops to mine. "I'm out of my element."

If this is out, I can't imagine in.

"You seem rightfully qualified to be my kissing instructor."

His chest moves as he takes deep breaths, and he runs a finger over my cheek. "I can't believe this is you. You're so beautiful."

"I'm not sure if that's a compliment."

Justin swallows, his Adam's apple bobbing. "It's meant as one. I keep reminding myself that you're…" He pauses. "That you've become more than Ricky's little tagalong sister."

"Tagalong?"

"Yeah," he says with a smirk.

"Well, I have to remind myself that you're more than Ricky's know-it-all, grumpy friend."

Justin takes a step back. "Is that what you think of me?"

"Past tense." I quickly add, "You called me a tagalong. We're even."

His stare is penetrating as if he's seeing behind my eyes into my soul. "I don't feel like we're even when I'm around you. I feel off-kilter."

"I'm sure you're more experienced at this than I am."

Justin shakes his head. "I don't recall ever feeling this way about a kiss. No one has ever annihilated my world with one kiss."

Taking a deep breath, I ask, "What does this mean?"

He shakes his head. "I don't know."

Lowering my chin, I sigh. When I look up, Justin is staring into my eyes. "Please don't be playing some kind of a joke."

"What?" His eyes grow wide. "Devan, I swear. I'm not."

"I don't think I could take it."

"Fuck," he hisses as his palm cups my cheek. "I don't

know what else you think of me or remember, but I'm not that person. If anything, I'm worried how Ricky will take it if you want to see me...like for real."

"Officially?"

Justin shrugs and nods.

I tip my head to his chest with my senses on high alert. The thumping of his heart, manly scent, solid muscular chest radiating warmth...the combination has me all jumbled. "Don't hurt me."

"That's the last thing I want to do."

Taking a deep breath, I smile. "When you're ready to officially ask me, I'll be waiting." I take a step away and grin. "Don't make me wait too long, Justin Sheers."

With that, I hurry across the gravel to my car and grab two suitcases from the back seat. I'm up on the porch when I hear Justin's truck door open. I turn in time to see him under the dome light. His auburn hair and scruff on his cheeks. His penetrating gaze, high cheekbones, and chiseled jaw.

My heart flutters at the thought of his kisses and touch.

It's my mind that has questions and worries.

I've never gone all the way.

The fact that I'm a virgin sounds archaic. I know my friends have, and that's fine. It's not that I have some old-fashion morality code. I think I want it to be special.

As I'm carrying my suitcases up the stairs, I'm worried that I don't know enough to keep a man like Justin Sheers happy.

Once I'm in my room with my door closed, I call Jill.

"Are you dying?" she asks in lieu of answering. "Why are you calling this late? Are your fingers broken? Text."

"I don't want any written record of this conversation," I say softly.

Jill's tone changes. "Oh, what are we going to talk about?"

"Sex."

"Should it be a video call? Do we need props?"

A laugh comes as my response. "What if I waited too long? What if I'm terrible at this?"

"Okay," Jill says. "I'm fully awake now. *This?* Did you see Justin again? Is he pushing you…? Talk to me."

"Yes. He's not. I think I need advice and help. That's why I called."

Chapter Fifteen

Justin

I pull my truck up to the middle school. While classes are out for the summer, there always seems to be a few cars. Devan says the janitorial staff is painting walls and replacing carpet squares. And then there are people like her, working to set up their classrooms. With the newer schedule, summer break isn't as long as I remember. Students will be back in the building by the end of July. That still gives Devan a little over six weeks to make her room exactly what she wants.

Yes, over the last few weeks, we've been talking, mostly on the phone, which she said is new for her. I'm curious what else is new for her. Checking my phone, I see the text message she sent earlier.

. . .

"COME IN TO THE SCHOOL. I WANT TO SHOW YOU SOMETHING. TEXT AND I'LL COME OPEN THE DOOR."

Unable to resist, I send a reply.

"TELL ME WHAT YOU WANT TO SHOW ME." Winking face emoji.

Devan doesn't take the bait. She replies.

"ARE YOU HERE?"

Instead of texting, I hit the call button. Devan answers on the first ring. "You are old. No one calls." Her voice is light, sweet, and enthusiastic, so I'm going to ignore the comment about my age.

"I'm in the parking lot."

It's great to hear the happiness in her voice. Last week, when she first visited the school, she was devastated that her classroom was an empty shell. Even the posters and charts she'd seen at the time of her interview were gone.

"I'm headed toward the front doors," she says.

Stepping out of my truck, I glance around the parking lot. At this time of evening, the paved lot has few cars. And the nearby baseball field has only a sparse number of kids on it. While part of me is ready to make things official with Devan, as of yet we're keeping our relationship a secret. In a small town, that's no easy feat.

Peering through the glass doors, I catch the last few seconds of Devan's approach. She positively bounces down the hallway and through the first set of doors. Her stunning smile brightens to a radiant glow as she pushes the bar on the outside door. Her cheeks are pink, and her long hair is in one braid that goes down the middle of her back. She's wearing a spaghetti-strap sundress that shows less leg than her shorts a few weeks ago. With her flat sandals, Devan is easily ten inches shorter than I.

Opening the door, she cranes her neck until I see the soft suede of her eyes. "Hi." Her volume is low and sexy.

"Hi," I say, my voice coming out huskier than usual.

"You're all cleaned up."

She is right.

After I got done working, I took a shower and even shaved. Today I spent most of the day working on our old tractor. My nails became filthy with grease as I got the tractor's timing back on par. Getting a new tractor isn't an expense I want if we're considering buying the Dunn farm.

It's odd but that possibility isn't something Devan and I have talked about. Mostly, I'm afraid she doesn't know that her dad is considering selling. I don't want to be the one to tell her.

"I figured you deserved the showered version."

Devan grins. "I'll take any version. The showered one smells good."

Yes, I added a splash of cologne.

I'm dying to cup her cheek and taste her sweet lips. Looking around at the empty offices, I consider my next move.

Before I can do anything, Devan reaches for my hand. "Come to my room."

"I wish you were inviting me to your bedroom," I whisper. My comment gets me a side look and a smile.

Devan leads me through the different hallways. This is only my second time to her classroom, and in a few minutes, I'm hopelessly lost. I would need a compass and the GPS on my phone to make it back to the front doors. Honestly, all my personal memories of middle school have been lost. It's like the entire file folder has been deleted. If I wasn't certain I've lived in Riverbend my entire life, I'd think a new school had been built. It hadn't. Renovation and additions have taken place. The temperature is too warm, no doubt saving money on the air conditioning.

With each step, I feel perspiration form on my skin.

"Look," she says, motioning into her classroom with her arm.

I take a step inside. Two large fans circulate the warm

air, creating a breeze. The desks have all been arranged with the big one at the front of the class.

No longer are the walls bare. There are bright posters with diagrams of cells, and inverted triangles with scientific and biological classification. The bulletin boards that were empty are covered in brightly colored papers. As I turn, I see the bookcases that were filled with only dust now hold textbooks.

"Damn," I say, making a complete circle. "Miss Dunn, you amaze me."

"I contacted Mrs. Scudder. Remember her?"

My head shakes. "I swear I must have slept through middle school."

Devan smiles. "She used to be the head of the science department. She retired a few years ago. Since John Jacobs took everything from the classroom, I wondered if she saved anything. Mr. Sams wasn't happy that it was all gone." Her nose scrunches. "I don't think Mr. Jacobs left on the best of terms."

"I didn't hear anything."

"It sounds like it was kept quiet."

"Cory is my friend," I say. "Why wouldn't he tell me?"

Devan puts her fist to her hip. "Why would he? Do you tell him when something goes wrong on the farm?"

"I tell anyone who will listen." As soon as the words leave my mouth, I laugh. "I get it. None of my business." My eyebrows move up. "Do you have the dirt?"

"Only rumors and I'm not going to be the one to

spread them. Anyway, not only did Mrs. Scudder have materials, but she was excited to get it out of her house." Devan practically floats to the front of the room. "And I found this website where I can download a pdf of posters. I then can have them printed for half the cost of the catalogue price and printed in any size." She motions toward the bookcases. "Mr. Sams found the textbooks. Mr. Jacobs had stuffed them in a custodial closet."

"There is definitely a story I need to learn."

Devan comes closer, taking both of my hands in hers and looking up at me. "The only story you need to know is that the new science teacher is getting excited for her first class. And nervous."

"You're going to be amazing. I just know it."

"I want to make the students love science as much as I do."

"Now, the rest of the summer you're free to..." I have a long list of things I'd like her to do.

"No," she says, shaking her head. "The textbook company has guides and lesson plans, but I need to go through each one. Did you know that nowadays, the entire semester syllabus is supposed to be online before the first day of school?"

"I didn't." It's not a lie. I have no idea what teachers do.

"I could simply post the one Mr. Jacobs used, but I need to be sure it covers all the standards, and I want to give it my personal touch."

I squeeze her hands. "With your touch, it will be

perfect." Letting go of her hand, I lift her chin, pressing a soft kiss to her sweet lips. "Dinner?"

"An official date? The diner on Main?"

"No." I quickly add, "Not because I'm not ready to make this public but because I have other plans."

Her face tilts as her brown eyes glisten. "What plans do you have, Justin?"

"A picnic. I thought we could drive to the quarry pits. Find a secluded spot, and..." —I lift my eyebrows— "eat."

Devan looks down at herself. "I've been working all day. I'm hot and sweaty and—"

"The most beautiful girl I know."

The pink hue in her cheeks reddens to a rosy glow. "Let me call my mom. I don't want her to expect me for dinner and I don't show."

"Is that a yes?"

"You packed a picnic?" she asks.

"I did. I can't promise it's great. If it's not edible, we can stop and get something."

"But *you* packed it?"

I nod. "I couldn't ask my mom to do it. She'd ask questions." I let out a sigh. "This may come as a shock, but I'm not exactly known for my romantic gestures."

Devan pushes up on her toes and brushes my lips with hers. "Yes, Justin Sheers, I will go on a picnic. I can't wait to see what you packed." Her hand goes over her stomach. "I've been working here since before lunch. I'm famished."

"Maybe we should go someplace closer."

Her gaze goes out the windows. "It's been a long time since I've been to the quarry pits. And it looks like a beautiful night." She sits behind the big desk at the front of the class.

While Devan looks more like a student than the teacher, I sense her pride and eagerness to take the role. As she speaks to her mom, I turn another full circle. The back of the classroom has small stations with sinks, places for students to conduct their own scientific experiments. In moments like these, I forget about our difference in age.

The annoying little girl has bloomed into a strong, intelligent, competent woman.

"...bye, Mom."

"Are you ready?" I ask.

Devan raises one finger and quickly sends a text message.

"Jill or Marilyn?" I ask, wondering which friend she contacted.

"Jill," she says with a grin. Grabbing her big bag, Devan leads me toward the door. "Who is your cover?"

"I don't have a cover," I answer honestly. "My folks don't ask. They probably think I'm with a list of different guys. And no one else keeps track of my coming and going."

Devan locks the door to her classroom. I follow her lead, hoping we won't need GPS to make it back to the front doors. When we get to the parking lot, her car is near my truck.

"Hide your car?" I ask.

She shakes her head. "I can say Jill picked me up. Just bring me back here after our picnic."

I open the passenger door to my truck. Devan reaches for the handle, steps on the running board, and climbs into the seat. Before I close the door, I stand, staring.

"What's wrong?" she asks.

"Nothing. I like having you in my truck."

She looks around. "It's big."

"I'm also thinking that I'd rather keep you than return you to your car."

Devan grins as she latches her seat belt. "Come on. I'm hungry."

"One more thing," I say, my confidence waning.

"What?"

I open the back door of the truck and lift the bouquet of daisies I picked for her. "I..." —I stammer— "...you said you like them."

Devan's eyes grow wide as she takes the flowers. "Justin, they're beautiful."

"Not as beautiful as you." I close the door, wondering if she thinks I sound ridiculous. It's not my goal, but as I said, this is uncharted territory. There's something about Devan that seems different—in a good way.

Opening the driver's door, I grin. "You think I'm corny?"

She shakes her head. "No, I don't." Her smile is gorgeous. "I think this is our first date." She looks at the flowers and back to me. "And if you don't get us to our picnic spot soon, I may have to eat the daisies."

Chapter Sixteen

Devan

Our first date.

Justin didn't deny it. The bouquet of fresh daisies on the seat between us and the fact I'm in his truck are both proof that it's real. Music blares from the speakers as he turns on the truck and rolls down the windows.

We don't talk as he drives us down Main Street on our way out of town. I barely move. My pulse is racing as we pass familiar stores, the diner, and Bob's, a local tavern. I feel like there's a spotlight on us, yet the people walking along the sidewalks don't seem to notice. The farther out of town we get, the more open fields and fewer structures we pass and the less my nerves are on edge.

Smiling, I lift my face to the breeze as his truck bounces along back roads toward Empire Quarry. Trees lining the roads are filled with green leaves. The world is alive with summer growth. The quarry where we're going is near Bedford. It got its name because it's famous for providing the nearly twenty thousand tons of limestone needed to construct the Empire State Building.

My science geek comes out as I start thinking about the composition of limestone, a sedimentary rock principally composed of calcium carbonate or calcite and aragonite, a crystal form of calcium carbonate. Tiny fossils, shell fragments, and debris are also often found within it.

Justin turns the radio down and grins. "What are you thinking?"

I laugh. "You don't want to know."

"I do."

"I was thinking about the quarry and the composition of limestone. Did you know that most of the limestone was formed by either a chemical or biochemical process that occurred about 300 million years ago?"

He turns my direction, his eyes huge.

Covering my face, I laugh. "Sorry. I'm a science geek. I love earth science."

"I did know that...about the composition, not that you love earth science."

"You did?"

"Yeah, while my major at Purdue was agriculture and I also studied business, my favorite subject was geology."

"Really?" I asked, surprised.

"Yeah, well, I don't often throw around my geological knowledge. If I did, I'd have every woman in Indiana after me."

"You would. It's damn sexy to hear a guy talk about the lithosphere, mantle, outer core, and inner core."

Justin laughs. "You're giving away your secrets. You want a man who can recite the chemical composition and minerals in the lithosphere."

"You definitely have me figured out."

"Have you ever gone swimming in the quarries?" he asks.

I turn his direction. "Don't tell me your plans for tonight include swimming. I didn't bring a swimsuit."

His smile quirks. "That wasn't my plan, but it's sounding better all the time."

"I only swam in a quarry once. It was up at Sanders Quarry." I shiver. "People were jumping off the rooftop."

Justin's eyes open wide as he turns from the road to me and back. "Did you jump?"

"No," I say definitively with a shake of my head. "I wouldn't say I'm afraid of heights, but plunging from seventy feet in the air into water surrounded by some of the hardest rock formations around isn't my idea of fun."

"I did it," Justin admits. "And if you tell Ricky what I'm about to say, I'll never share another secret."

Warmth fills my cheeks that Justin wants to share a secret. I lift my right hand. "I swear."

His strong hands grip the steering wheel. "It was one summer after high school. Cory had been in Bloomington for school. I think it was after our freshman year. I had been up in West Lafayette. He and I got into a Purdue versus IU debate, and Cory dared us to go up to Bloomington to Sanders Quarry. The place was packed."

"Despite the no-trespassing signs," I add, remembering them from when I was there.

"Right." He sighs. "Cory was the first to jump." He turns my direction. "I'm not afraid of heights."

"I believe you."

"Then Galvin and Nick jumped. I was next, and I swear to God, I was scared shitless. Those few seconds when you're in the air and the limestone wall is right there..." He shakes his head. "When we all climbed out, everyone was saying how fun it was." He turns my way. "Yeah, not fun."

I can't help but laugh. "You went further than I did. I swam, but not by jumping off the rooftop. And it was cold."

"Freezing."

"Can I assume there's no swimming in tonight's plans?"

"We could go to Lake Monroe one day. The water is a lot warmer."

I like that he's talking about the future. "That would be nice."

Justin pulls his truck along the side of a back road. The tires crunch the gravel beneath. "It's not too long of a walk from here."

I'm wearing a dress and sandals, not exactly hiking apparel, and yet in that moment, I'm willing to follow Justin Sheers anywhere. A few minutes later, with a picnic basket in one hand and a blanket draped over his shoulder, Justin offers me his hand. Looking down at his wide palm and outstretched fingers, I smile, my gaze going back to his blue eyes. "You want to hold my hand?"

He shrugs. "I don't want you to fall. The path is kind of narrow."

Laying my hand in his, I watch as his fingers surround it and decide I know.

I'll follow Justin anywhere he leads me.

His touch is warm and steady. The strength I witnessed as he lifted boxes and furniture is still present, only gentler and more protective. Not only is he ten years older than I, but he's also much taller and wider, making me feel safe from whatever or whomever we could cross along our journey.

He was right. The path is narrow with long grass and saplings on each side. We walk in and out of the shadows of tall trees as chipmunks, squirrels, and other small crea- tures scatter in the underbrush and birds watch us from branches high above. When we emerge from the trees, we're atop a flat sheet of limestone, probably twenty feet wide. At the other side is a drop off. The turquoise-blue water of the quarry is below.

Justin releases my hand, and I turn a complete circle. The green leaves against the sapphire sky sway in the summer breeze. And within the quarry down below, the water is still, not a ripple mars it, creating a mirror of the scene above. "This is beautiful. How did you find this spot?"

Justin lays out the blanket and shrugs. "I've been here before."

"With another girl?" The question slips out before I can stop it. "Never mind."

"Yes," he says. "I'm not going to lie to you, Devan. That said, it was a long time ago." He sits on the blanket. "I remembered this place." He looks around. "How secluded and nice it is here." His blue orbs meet mine. "And I wanted to share it with you."

I sit near him, both of us facing the water. The rock's warmth penetrates the material. "It's okay." I turn to him with a grin. "I'm glad you want to share it with me. I guess I'm surprised there aren't more people here."

He lies back, propping his elbow on the blanket and holding up his head. His sexy blue stare is focused on me in a way that makes me warm and covers me with goose bumps at the same time.

His deep voice is smooth and easy. "It's because the access road for the quarry is a few miles from where I parked. It's blocked by a locked gate and has big no-trespassing signs. The way we came in...not a lot of people know about it."

"We're trespassing?" I ask. "Could we be arrested?"

Justin smirks. "More likely we'd be told to leave. I think there are more pressing crimes for the police or sheriff to worry about." He winks. "Don't worry. If it happens, I'll take full blame. I kidnapped you."

"I went willingly."

I'm struck by how handsome I think Justin is. With his long legs covered by blue jeans and his blue t-shirt stretched over his wide chest, he has a rugged appearance. The way his arm is flexed shows the bulge of muscle in his bicep. His auburn hair is no longer damp but messy and windblown from our drive. And under the summer sky, his eyes are strikingly blue.

"I can't believe you wanted to bring me here," I finally say.

He pushes himself up to sitting and leans closer. After only a second's hesitation, his lips come to mine. Our bodies are drawn to one another as our kiss deepens.

By the time we pull back for air, Justin laughs. "I'd like to keep kissing you." His smile grows. "But from the sounds of your stomach, I should feed you first."

Laughing, I cover my stomach with my hands. "That's so embarrassing."

"I think it's cute."

Great.

Cute.

After opening the picnic basket, Justin starts to remove the contents when he catches my expression. "What did I say?"

"You said I'm cute, as in a puppy."

"Oh fuck no. You're cute as in perfect, stunning, gorgeous, and you take my breath away." Setting down a container, he reaches for my hand. "I'm not the best with words, but you can be assured cute will never be meant as a derogatory term. And... I adore puppies. So, no, not a bad analogy."

I have the flash of an image of grumpy Justin Sheers on the floor with a puppy, laughing and playing. Shaking that imagery away, I open the plastic container and find fresh strawberries. Plucking one from the bowl, I put it in my mouth. The sweet fruit bursts with juice. "Mmmm. It's delicious."

His voice is deep. "I'm suddenly thinking things I shouldn't about you and those strawberries."

My cheeks warm.

He goes on, removing more things from the basket. "Full disclosure, I didn't cook the strawberries. I didn't really cook." After removing paper plates, plastic ware, and napkins, he pulls out two sandwiches. I recognize the paper as from the local deli. "Turkey or roast beef?"

"Both," I say.

Justin opens the paper and places one half of the turkey on one plate and the other half on the other. He does the same with the roast beef.

My mouth is watering and my stomach's still growling. "Condiments?"

He removes individual packets of ketchup and mustard. His stare meets mine with a devilish grin. "Did I forget something?"

I work to hide my disappointment. Shaking my head, I reach for a ketchup. "No. This is great."

Next, he pulls out a bag of potato chips.

As I'm about to tear open the ketchup packet, I'm struck by a flying packet. "What?" I pick up the small blue foil. "Mayo."

His smile blooms. "I got the feeling that day when we were packing your apartment that you liked mayonnaise."

Tossing the ketchup aside, I eagerly tear open the packet he'd tossed my way. "I do."

He remembered.

The bottom layer of the basket is a cooler. Justin removes two bottles of water and a bottle of wine. It's a blush from a local winery. His lopsided grin quirks. "I don't know if you like wine. And I promise, I'm not trying to get you intoxicated. There's always water."

"I like wine, especially from Oliver winery."

Justin is prepared with a wine opener. As he pulls the cork, he explains, "My mom likes wine. I'm more of a beer guy."

"I like both."

He pours wine into two plastic cups and lifts his in the air. "To one kiss."

We tap our cups.

The wine is light and fruity, perfect for a summer evening. We talk as we eat, about nothing and everything.

"How do you feel about baseball?" Justin asks.

Shrugging, I reply, "Unless it's the Red Sox, I'd rather watch Riverbend play softball."

His nose scrunches. "I was afraid of that."

"Not a Red Sox fan?"

"I cheer for local teams, and since Indiana doesn't have a major league team that leaves St. Louis."

"Or Cincinnati or Chicago," I say with a grin.

His smirk grows. "Challenge accepted. I will turn you into a Cardinals fan yet."

"Pretty sure of yourself. My whole family cheers for the Red Sox."

He shakes his head. "And here I thought you were perfect." His smile grows. "I guess this makes you nearly perfect."

At first, I thought it was odd talking at night on the phone to one another, but in hindsight, it's made both of us more comfortable around each other. When there is silence, it's not awkward.

Justin has said more than once that he feels out of his element. Yet I don't sense that. The drive, walk through the woods, and picnic destination are perfect in every way. He tells me about Quintessential Treasures, a store his sister owns in Riverbend. I've been in the store a hundred times. However, not recently. He talks about changes she's made in the last few years since Ruth Richards passed away.

Listening to Justin Sheers speak about his sister with pride is another unexpected surprise. It's when he mentions his niece, Molly, that his entire countenance lightens.

"You really like being around her."

Smiling, he nods. "When I found out Kandace was

pregnant, I was pretty pissed off." He shakes his head. "Molly...the first time I held her, I knew she wasn't a mistake. I think Kandace and I got closer during those years. I know Mom misses having them living with us."

"Moms..." I sigh. Looking up at light, fluffy clouds high above, I say what I haven't said to anyone. "I'm worried my parents have put their dreams on hold for me." I turn to him. "I don't think anyone is supposed to know, but Ricky told me that they were talking about selling the farm."

Justin lets out a long breath. "I'm so glad you know."

"You know?"

"Ricky told me. I told your dad I don't want him to sell to that developer. I've offered to buy it."

"You what? When?"

Justin shakes his head. "It was before...before our kiss."

"In other words, you're not trying to buy my home because of our kiss."

"No, but that's a damn good reason." He leans closer, pushing my empty plate out of the way and brushes his lips with mine.

The energy we gained from our meal energizes me as I push toward him. His lips are full and strong. Like when he holds my hand, I feel safe and protected in his presence.

I fall back on the blanket, Justin follows, his face close to mine. Staring into his blue gaze, I say, "I think I need more practice."

He teases rogue strands of my long hair away from my face. "I want to make this official."

I nod.

"Ricky is probably going to hate me, but he'll hate both of us more if we don't tell him."

Stretching my neck, I kiss him again. "If you're asking if I want to date you, the answer is yes."

His smile grows. "No, Devan, that's not what I'm asking."

"You aren't?"

"I'm asking if you'll date *only* me. You see, I'm not great at this relationship thing. My track record is...well... mostly nonexistent. I also know that you blew me away that first night and every day since. I don't want to be clingy, but I can't imagine seeing you with someone else."

Words don't form for me. The world around us has stilled. Except, that is, for my heart that is fluttering out of control. All I can see is the depth in his eyes, the different shades of blue, much like that of the quarry below.

Justin continues talking. "Walking into your apartment and seeing you turned my world upside down." He swallows. "I thought I'd built that night—that kiss—up in my head. It was the night Ricky told me your parents were considering selling. I wasn't in a great mood. And then I saw you, started talking to you. You were beautiful, fun, and despite my bad mood, made me smile. And then you were gone. I tried to find out who you were, but no one knew you—no one remembered seeing you. I couldn't understand because you were all I remembered. Then I decided maybe you weren't real. I'd practically given up hope of ever seeing you again, and then there you were."

Chapter Seventeen

Justin

Closing my eyes, I lean my forehead to Devan's and exhale. This is too much, too soon. I shouldn't be as honest with her. It's that when I'm with her, I want to talk, share, and even be honest about my feelings. There is something about her that just feels right.

Devan's hands come to my cheeks as she lifts my face until our eyes meet. "Yes."

I let out the breath I'm holding. "Fuck, I was pretty sure that word-vomit would have sent you running."

"It wasn't vomit," she says with a soft laugh to her voice. "It was sweet and honest. I spent those next five weeks afraid that by coming back to Riverbend, I'd see you and you'd pretend you didn't know or recognize me." She tilts her head. "You did that."

I sit up, noticing how with Devan's golden hair around her face, she looks like an angel. "What was I supposed to do, make a scene in front of your dad and brother?"

"If we'd gone all that day without talking about it—the kiss—I know I wouldn't be here right now."

"Then I'm thankful for the breeze slamming the doors." I recall her excuse.

"And the fortuitous tote."

Yeah, I'm having the same problem again.

"Devan," I say, my voice an octave lower. "Come here."

I sense the way her breathing deepens by the way her breasts push against the front of her sundress.

"I'm here."

Tilting my head, I motion for her to come closer.

She moves to her knees and turns until we're facing one another, our knees touching. For longer than I meant to, I simply stare at her—the all of her. The beauty of her soft skin, the way her nose turns up, her perfect kissable lips, and the depth in her swirling chocolate eyes. The straps of her dress hang from her slender shoulders. If I sit taller, I could see down her neckline and from what I can see, I don't think she's wearing a bra. Going by the other night outside her house, I know how good it feels to be against her, to feel her warmth and soft curves.

I want to push those straps off her shoulders and see what she's wearing—or not wearing—beneath.

Taking a deep breath, I remember what I wanted to

say, to ask. "I've given this a lot of thought, and I don't know how to ask something without sounding like a dick."

Devan smiles. "Oh, what does a dick sound like?"

"A dick question," I explain, lifting her hands in mine. "I know you're not a kid. I know you've grown up and that's great. Fuck, it's better than great. Part of me wants to take everything slowly, but maybe that part of me doesn't know what you know." I shake my head again. "It doesn't matter if you've been with anyone else," I lie, because saying it aloud makes me realize it does matter. Instead, I go on, "What matters is that while we figure this out, we're exclusive."

She nods. "I've dated."

I nod, wanting more information.

"You've dated, I'm sure."

I nod again.

Yeah, that would mean information-sharing is a two-way street.

"You're asking me if I'm a virgin?"

"Yeah," I admit. "Dick question."

"It kind of is." Devan sits back, pulling her knees to her chest and wrapping her arms around them. "If I say I am, then I'm back to being a child in your eyes. If I say I'm not, I'm a slut."

"No." The one word comes out louder than I mean it to. "You're definitely not a slut. And I think we've established that you're not a kid. I just..." I take a deep breath. "I don't want to fuck this up. I'm willing to take it slow if that's what you want. And if you want to go faster, I'm game with that too. I guess I thought that having that knowledge would give me an idea on the speed."

Devan relaxes her knees and lays her fingers on my arm. Her touch is warm and soft. Slowly, she moves her gaze from where we're touching to my face. "I don't know what speed I want. I like when you kiss me and when you touch me."

Tugging on her hand, I coax her to come even closer.

"Justin."

"I'm not pushing."

"No," she says with a grin. "You're pulling."

"I want to touch you."

Slowly, she nods and moves closer.

I'm seated with my legs out in a V and Devan settles on my lap, facing me with her legs bent around my waist and her hands on my shoulders. I hold onto her waist as her pussy hovers over my trapped erection.

Her eyes are wide, and I know she can feel what is happening to me.

With my gaze on hers, I tease one strap of her dress from her shoulder. When she doesn't stop me, I tease the other. The front of her dress settles just over her perfect tits—no bra—giving me a slight peek at the deep pink of her areolas.

My lips pepper her soft flesh.

First, her lips, then down to her neck, and her collarbone. I'd gotten this far the other night. Today,

I continue lower and lower until my chin nudges her dress down, and I suck one nipple and then the other.

"Justin."

The way she says my name combined with the way her body fidgets in my grasp has me ready to come in my jeans. "Tell me to stop," I say between kisses.

Her fingers weave through my hair, her breaths come more rapidly, and her back arches to give me better access. "Don't stop," she pants.

I work her arms from the straps, leaving her dress more like a skirt—from the waist up, she's exposed. My fingers splay and caress, tracing the arch of her spine as her nipples bead and she fidgets in my lap. I long to touch every inch of her, to know what turns her on and what she likes.

Back and forth, her pussy rubs over my jeans.

Slow, I remind myself.

It takes all my self-control not to free my erection and let her ride me.

This isn't about me. I lower my hands to her round ass, the one bouncing on top of me as I gather the material of her dress. It's as my fingers brush the edge of her panties that I stop.

Devan's eyes open wide.

"Do you want to come?" I ask.

Her lips press together as she nods.

"Don't be shy. What do you want?" I continue brushing the crotch of her panties.

"Oh." She drops her forehead to my shoulder. "This feels so good."

"What do you want?" I ask again.

"I want to come."

"Do you want me to help?"

"Yes," she says in a soft squeak of a voice.

"My fingers, my tongue, or you can keep dry humping me. Either way, I promise you'll come."

Indecision swirls in her eyes as her cheeks go from pink to flaming red.

Leaning back on my arms, I press my erection against her. "Dry hump. I want to watch you."

"No," she says quickly. "Your fingers."

"Good girl. Tell me what you want." A smile curls my lips as I readjust. "I'm still going to watch, Devan. You're too fucking gorgeous not to watch."

The material of her panties between her legs is soaked as I push it aside. Slickness covers my fingers as I tease the seam of her lower lips. My heart is racing as I find her core. Shit, she's so tight. Her walls clamp around my finger as she presses upward. It's as I swirl her clit with my thumb that she begins to moan and gasp for air.

"Press back on my hand, Devan."

She does as I say, and her moans morph to whimpers as her movements come faster. I add another finger, stretching her core and press my thumb against her clit. It's as if I've found her detonation button. Her body quakes in my grasp, her core convulses around my fingers, and her warm essence covers my hand. There are red areas on her skin from my facial hair, and her nipples are as hard as diamonds.

Devan lets her forehead drop to my shoulder as she rides out her orgasm and works to regain her normal breathing.

Removing my fingers, I bring them to my lips and suck.

Shaking her head, she keeps her eyes down.

"Damn, I knew you would be sweet as candy."

"I can't believe I did that." Her voice is muffled by my shoulder. "We did."

"Devan, look at me."

Her brown orbs come into view. Quickly, I press my lips to hers. "You can't believe you just came on my hand."

"Yeah," she says shyly. "I've never come that hard. Ever."

She leans back. Either she's forgotten that she's still naked from the waist up or she doesn't care. "What about you?" she asks.

"What about me?"

"That...it was for me. Don't you want to...?"

My gaze scans from her tousled hair, pink cheeks, down to her perfect hand-sized tits, and back to her eyes. "I want to. But tonight is about you. I want you to know you will always be my first thought. I'll never force you, Devan."

"We're really going to do this?" she asks.

"This?" My grin quirks. "Yeah, you can come on my hand anytime, any day."

"Date," she says, slapping my shoulder.

"Exclusive," I say. "I've tasted you, and I don't want anyone else tasting or touching what's mine."

"And it goes both ways?"

"Are you asking if I'm yours?"

"I am."

"For as long as you'll have me." I think about that for a moment. As I'm helping Devan with her dress, I add, "Unless Ricky kills me first."

Chapter Eighteen

Devan

After Justin readjusts my dress, I settle between his legs, my back against his chest as we sit on the blanket and watch as the sky fills with purples and reds. The effects of what he did isn't gone. It's as if mini explosions are still detonating beneath my skin like firecrackers in a string, bringing life to nerve endings I never knew existed. His heart pounds against my head, and I feel him everywhere. Craning my neck, I look back at him. "After what we did" —I'm still in shock — "I think we need to make this officially real."

His hand settles on my stomach, his fingers splayed. "I think that's what we just did."

"I'm talking about telling people."

"I agree." He lifts my chin so I'm looking back at him. "We could tell your family tonight."

My eyes open wide. "You'd be willing to tell them *tonight*?"

"Is that too fast?"

I chew on my upper lip. "I don't know. Why is this complicated?" I sigh, laying my hand over his. "What will your family say?"

Justin laughs. "My mom will probably ask when I'm moving out."

"Yeah, no. Cohabitation is rushing it a bit." Earlier today, I would have said that Justin fingering me was rushing it. Obviously, I'm not a good judge of timing.

"Seriously," he says, "my parents are good people. I think their first reaction will be shock. I'm certain they think I'm a hermit. I haven't dated a lot since college."

"Why?"

"Fuck." He turns his hand so we're palm to palm. "Riverbend."

"I don't understand. I thought you said you always knew you were coming back to Riverbend."

"I did. Not many women want to move to some rural town when they have career ambitions." He quickly adds, "Your ambitions are fantastic, and they brought you back."

Nodding, I reply, "I get it."

"And once I came back, the girls I knew were either married or moved away. I'd say I've gotten into a rut with friends. It's not a bad one. It's comfortable, and I haven't looked for a way out."

"That's why you're worried about Ricky?"

Justin's chest moves as he inhales and exhales. "I'm worried that if you and I don't work out, I'll lose you and him."

I squeeze his hand. "How come I never realized how sweet you are?"

"Because you thought I was a grumpy know-it-all."

"Well, you can be that too." I lift my head and turn toward him. "Are you friends with your brother-in-law?"

He scoffs. "Now."

"But not before he came back to Riverbend?" I may have been in Muncie, but small-town news has a way of finding those with a stake in our hometown.

"No, I wanted to kill him." He grins. "I did punch him."

I stifle a laugh. "Because you saw Kandace hurt?"
He nods.

"Don't hurt me, Justin Sheers. We can work out or maybe we won't. Just don't hurt me, and you won't lose Ricky."

Justin cups my cheek and moves my face closer. "I don't want to hurt you, Devan. I want to make every damn dream you have come true. I want to hold your hand when we walk, to give you the strength you need to be the best you and get that same in return."

He lands a soft kiss on my lips.

I'm thinking about telling my family.

"Tomorrow," I say. "I think I know a way to make it go over better. If I'm right, you can come back to our house for dinner tomorrow."

He looks worried. "Are they going to make me eat hot sauce...you know some hazing thing?"

My laugh fills the air. "No, that hot sauce is horrible."

"It is." He lifts my hand to his lips. "I'm laying it all out on the table. I want to do more than tell you how much I like you. I want to show you like I did tonight and more. I want to show you what your kisses do to me."

I nod. It's what I want too.

"Speed?" he asks.

"Let's make it through being official, and then we can get back to your dick question."

He smirks. "My dick is the one asking."

It is also still hard beneath his jeans. I again lay my head against his chest and stare out at the sky. Even though the sun isn't fully set, the moon is out, low on the horizon. "It's more common to see the sun and moon at the same time than for the moon to be alone."

"Most visible during a full moon," he says.

We go on talking about the moon and its rotation as if it were a normal subject. And with Justin it does feel normal. I like that he can converse about things I like, things my friends often call boring.

"That night," I say, "the one of our first kiss, you asked me if I could see the man in the moon. It's a good thing I didn't bore you with the topography of the moon's surface and what makes the illusion of a face visible."

"It is. If you would have, I would have been a goner." He holds me to his front. "I am, Devan. I'm a goner."

"Tell me about what you do."

"I plant seed, tend to crops, harvest, sell, and do it again."

"You make it sound so exciting," I say with a laugh.

"It can be."

Again, I turn to see his handsome face. "I know that. I lived with it all my life. Real farmers do more than what you just said. It's a respect for the land, for what it can give us and what we need to give back. I think my dad started my love of science."

As the dark ink of night bleeds over the colorful hues of the setting sun, Justin and I gather up our picnic, what's left of our food and wine, and take it to the truck. It's as we're nearing the middle school that I ask one more time. "Are you sure you're ready to be official?"

"I'm beginning to think that you're the one who isn't."

"No, I am."

He turns and smirks my direction. "You are because you like the way I kiss or how I can make you come?"

My fingers go to my face as my cheeks warm. "Both. Could we please not keep talking about the latter?"

"You said if I hadn't mentioned the kiss at your apartment, we wouldn't be here."

"Right," I say, nodding. "Let's talk about that."

His blue eyes reflect the lights of his dashboard as he

grins. "Okay. Just to clarify, it's how sweet you taste that you don't want to talk about."

Instead of answering, I collect the daisies. Their petals are closed and the stems limp. "I'll put these in water when I get home. They'll be rigid again in no time."

"I know how they feel."

"If you say things like that around Ricky, he will punch you."

"Devan, I'm not a guy who talks about what's private and what's his. I enjoy watching you blush. What we do isn't anyone else's business."

"I'll text you later," I say as he pulls his truck next to my car. "I need to test the waters, but I think my plan will work."

When I start to open the door, Justin tells me to stop. I shake my head as he hurries from his side and gets to my door, opening it for me and offering me his hand.

"I also take care of what is mine." He lifts my hand to his lips. "Are you sure it's too soon to talk cohabitation? My mom will be thrilled if I move out."

"Too soon," I say, ready to brush his scruffy cheek with a kiss.

Justin redirects my face, so instead of kissing his cheek, our lips come together.

After all we shared tonight, the good-night kiss is supposed to be anticlimactic, but it isn't. My body goes slack against the firmness of his chest, melding against him as his palm tilts my face and my lips bruise.

"Good night, Devan."

His deep tenor rumbles through me.

"Good night, Justin."

As I drive toward my house, I'm surprised to see how late it has become. This time of year, the sun sets later at night. I cut my lights as I approach the garages, fearful I'll wake my parents. My car is the only one missing, meaning everyone else is home. Despite the late hour, the back door is unlocked as I slip into the kitchen, latching the door behind me.

The kitchen is illuminated by the blue light of a contraption Mom says is supposed to catch bugs. Quietly, I open the cupboard above the microwave and pull down a vase. After filling it with water, I begin to put the daisies in when I turn to footsteps coming from the back stairs.

"They'll do better," Mom says, "if you cut the ends. Unless they were just picked."

I go to the junk drawer and find a pair of scissors. "Thanks. They were picked earlier tonight."

Wearing her bathrobe, Mom comes to my side and helps me arrange the daisies. "They're very pretty."

I nod.

"That was nice of Jill to give you flowers."

I turn, meeting her gaze. "You know I wasn't with Jill?"

Her lips curl upward. "I do now. Do you want to talk?"

"I could use your help."

Chapter Nineteen

Justin

The round table at the back of the Main Street Diner is nearly filled with guys close to my age. Some are older, like Harvey and Galvin, while others are younger, like Nick. Despite today's crowd, there's still one empty chair when I arrive. As soon as I sit, Joyce, our favorite waitress and the owner of the diner, places a cup of black coffee in front of me. "What can I get you, Justin?"

I look around the table seeing that some of the other guys have food. "The morning platter. Over medium with sausage, potatoes, and an English muffin."

She grins. "Coming right up." Next, she points across the table to Cory who's sitting with Dax, my brother-in-law. "Your food is up. I'll be right back." She addresses the entire table. "More coffee?"

Different people nod. Some hold up their cups.

This gathering is a weekday morning ritual. There can be as many as ten squeezed around the table or as few as four. No matter who shows, we know we'll have a few minutes of downtime and conversation with friends. As I lift my coffee to my lips, I listen to Ricky talking about the summer softball season. I hate to admit it, but we've gotten better since my brother-in-law came back to town.

Of course, I'd deny that statement to most of my friends.

"First game is tonight," Ricky says.

My stomach drops.

I woke to a text from Devan saying her plan is in motion and to be at her house by six for dinner. "Fuck," I growl. "I forgot."

"Like you have plans..." Ricky says.

"Maybe he has a date," Cory says nonchalantly.

"I just forgot. I might not be able to make it."

"It doesn't start until eight thirty," Dax chimes in. "We're the late game."

"Oh yeah," I say, "I can make the late game."

Ricky looks at me funny, or I imagine he does.

By the time my food arrives, we're talking smack about the team from Mitchell. If our predictions go as mapped out, Cory will pitch a no-hitter, and we're going to smoke those guys so badly that the game will end mercy rule.

"Don't forget to wear your orange Riverbend shirt."

Nick turns to me. "If it's still stuffed in your ball bag since the end of last season, do us all a favor and wash it."

Everyone laughs, including me. Yes, I've been known to do that. It is usually only one week but the stink factor is strong. "Hey," I say, "that's my secret weapon. Stink the other team out."

Keeping my eye on Ricky, I try to sense if anything is off. I'm being paranoid, but the truth is that I had a great time with Devan last night. I did take a long, cold shower when I got home, but that doesn't lessen the enjoyment for the evening. I'm nervous about how dinner will go tonight.

It doesn't seem as though he even knows I've been invited.

I don't say anything about it because Devan said she has a plan.

"See you tonight," Dax says, standing. He's the first to leave. Since he's wearing a dress suit and pants, it means he'll be spending the day doing legal or title work. Cory too, is dressed nice for work, heading to the middle school, despite the students being out for the summer. Nick is wearing a shirt with his name over the pocket. Harvey, Ricky, and I are in jeans and t-shirts, looking as if we have a day of hard labor in our future.

Soon, the table is down to Cory and me. Being the last to arrive, I'm still finishing my breakfast. "I'm good," I say with a smirk and another bite of potatoes. "You don't need to wait for me. After this, I'm headed to Terre Haute to pick up some hybrid seed."

Cory nods, picks up his cup of coffee, and before taking another drink, peers toward the door. Once the last two guys to get up from the table leave the diner, filling the air with the ringing of the bell over the door, Cory sets his cup down. "I don't know what your plans are," he says softly, "but unless you want Ricky to take you down, be more careful."

I lower my fork to my plate.

My appetite disappears with Cory's warning.

"What are you talking about?" I ask, despite the fact I know what he's saying.

"Last night after the kids went to sleep, I went over to the school to grab something I forgot." He lifts his eyebrows. "Ringing any bells?"

"Is there some rule against teachers on school grounds after hours?" The small hairs on the back of my neck are standing on end.

"No, teachers can be there. It's frowned upon for them to be making out in the parking lot."

My tone lowers to a growl. "If there's a problem, bring it to me. Devan didn't do anything wrong."

"I am, Justin. Shit, I don't care what my teachers do in their private time as long as it's legal. Just do it in private. Not in the school parking lot."

That makes me wonder about the guy Devan is replacing. Before I can ask, Cory goes on.

"I don't want parents to complain, and if they saw what I saw last night, they would."

"I fucking kissed her goodbye." It was hardly an X-rated moment.

"She's new, and new teachers have to prove themselves, even Riverbend RTSers."

"She will," I say, my need to defend Devan fueling my words. "You should see her classroom. One kiss shouldn't sway anyone's opinion. Let her work do that."

"What about her age?" he asks.

"She's legal." I use his own word.

Cory sits back and shakes his head. "Does Ricky know?"

"We're telling him tonight."

Cory snorts and tips his face down. "Well, there goes our team unity."

"I forgot about the game. Devan has a plan, and it includes me going to dinner at the Dunns' home tonight."

"Well, if you show up tonight with a shiner, I'll know where it came from—or who."

* * *

"ARE YOU STILL EXPECTING ME?"

I ask in a text to Devan later in the day as I head toward my house. I have an hour to clean up. Waiting for her response makes me realize how Cory's confrontation this morning has fucked with me.

I thought our only obstacles would be Jack and Ricky. Maybe I didn't think the whole thing through enough.

'What about her age?' His question has been eating at me all day.

What the fuck difference does it make about her age or mine?

My phone dings as I step onto the porch. The text is from Devan.

"YES. COME BY A LITTLE BEFORE SIX. MOM SAID DINNER IS EARLIER BECAUSE RICKY HAS A GAME. ARE YOU GOING TO PLAY?"

I text back, her question reminding me of my orange shirt.

"I FORGOT ABOUT IT UNTIL THIS MORNING AT BREAKFAST. IF RICKY DOESN'T KILL ME FIRST, I'LL PLAY."

She responds with a heart and then a text message.

"I WILL PLAN ON WATCHING."

. . .

Fuck.

I wipe my palm over my face as I enter the kitchen, my thoughts torn between wanting to make things official and ready to hide us forever from judgy people—like the entire population of Riverbend.

"Justin," Mom says as I turn to go up the back stairs.

"Hey, Mom." I furrow my brow. "Do you remember seeing my softball shirt?"

"Not for a couple weeks."

"Tonight is the first game of the new season. I'm worried it's in the bottom of my bag."

"Oh Lord. If it is, it may be beyond repair."

I scoff. "Thanks for the support."

"What time is the game? I could wash it. You better check."

Standing on the bottom step, I meet my mom's gaze. "Where's Dad?"

"Today is Thursday. After working, he went to Washington to bowl."

Yeah. I forgot.

To say I've been distracted would be an understatement.

"Honey," Mom asks, "is everything all right? I mean about more than your shirt."

Letting out a breath, I step back down to the kitchen floor. "What if I told you something about me?"

Mom pulls out a chair at the table and sits. "Justin

Mathew, there is nothing you can tell me that will make me love you less."

"It's not that big," I say as I take the seat at the end of the table. "In a way, it might be…"

She lays her hand on the table toward me. "What is it?"

I shrug. "I'm dating someone."

Mom's eyes open wide. "You are? Do I know this person?"

"Kind of. She just moved back to Riverbend."

Mom's smile broadens. "Do you like her?"

"I do."

"Does she like you?"

"I think she does. I asked her last night to be exclusive."

"And she isn't ready for that?" Mom asks with her forehead furrowed.

"No, she said yes. I guess I'm worried. I don't want the fact she's dating me to fuck up her job or anything." Opening my eyes wide, I add, "Sorry."

"I've heard the word fuck before. What would make you think that dating you would be an issue with her job. What does she do?"

"She's a teacher. The new seventh-grade science teacher."

Mom tilts her head. "I thought little Devan Dunn was hired for that position—" Her eyes widen to the size of saucers. "Devan Dunn?"

I nod.

"Oh, Justin. What about Ricky?"

"He doesn't know yet. He will. Devan has a plan to tell her family tonight."

"I still don't understand how dating you and Devan's job are connected."

For the next few minutes, I recount my earlier conversation with Cory. "Do you think our age difference is too much? Will parents of her students judge her?"

My mom smiles as she leans back against the chair. "The fact that you're concerned about her and how people will perceive your relationship tells me all I need to know. You care about her."

"I do."

"What is your gut telling you?" Mom asks.

"To suck it up, go over to the Dunns', and take whatever Ricky and Jack want to give me."

"And at the game tonight?"

"I want to hold her hand and kiss her lips. I want the world to know she's mine."

"Because that makes you special?"

I think about her question. "No, because she is special."

Mom's grin returns. "Justin, people will judge. It's wrong and goes against what we've been taught, but it's human nature. I'm sure that despite giving Devan the job, Cory sees her as Ricky's little sister. You don't. Your view will either change others' views or their views won't matter."

"What if they matter to Devan?"

"I think that's a conversation for the two of you to discuss."

"What about you?" I ask.

"Me. I want nothing more in life than for my children to be happy. If Devan is your person, your one... then I'm thrilled you found one another."

Sighing, I push the chair back with my feet and stand. "Thanks, Mom."

"Justin, tell Devan I said I'm happy, and I hope to get to know her."

"I will."

Chapter Twenty

Devan

The aroma of roasted chicken fills the kitchen as I stir the potatoes. Sticking a fork into one, I announce, "I think they're ready to mash."

Mom turns from where she's cutting fruit for a fruit salad. "Do you want to mash them?"

I scrunch my nose. "Ricky will complain about lumps."

Mom's smile grows. "If that's the only thing your brother complains about during the meal, we'll be getting off easy."

"You're right. Maybe lumps will distract him."

Removing the colander from the cupboard, I put it in the sink. Using hot pads, I carry the pan to the sink, and pour the potatoes and water into the strainer.

As I'm working, Mom brings a stick of butter and a carton of heavy cream and places them beside me.

"I see we're not going for the low-fat version."

"Honey, if there's one thing I've learned over the years is men like your dad, brother, and Justin Sheers work hard all day. Those calories go to energy, not to fat. Besides, if there are going to be lumps, they might as well be delicious lumps."

She's right.

One time, Marilyn and I tried a food delivery service. They sent all the fixings for a meal. All we had to do was cook it. The directions for their mashed potatoes had potatoes, water, and sour cream. In a nutshell, the final product was gross.

The whip of the hand mixer jiggles my hand as the blades scrape against the side of the pan. I'm concentrating on the lumps while adding butter and cream when suddenly, I stop. Swallowing, I turn toward the back door.

"Hey," Ricky calls. "I'm going to shower. I've got a softball game tonight." He doesn't stop or turn toward us as his voice fades away on the second floor.

My gaze meets Mom's.

Without a word, she comes to me and reaches for my arm. "Don't be worried, Devan. You're a grown woman. You can make your own choices."

Setting the hand mixer beside the pan, I cross my arms over my chest as tears threaten to ruin the small amount of makeup I put on for tonight's dinner-slash-confrontation.

"Are you changing your mind?" Mom asks.

Last night, I told her the whole story. I left out a few details, especially about what happened last night at Empire Quarry; nevertheless, I started with the kiss the night of the hog roast. She was disappointed to learn I'd been in town without telling her. Yet in the grand scheme of our discussion, that topic received minimal attention. Mostly, I told her how I feel being with Justin. I mentioned his immense skill in the kissing department. I also told her about our evening telephone chats, the way he held my hand, and that he asked me to date exclusively.

According to Mom, she knew that there was someone in my life before I told her. She's noticed my smile and something different about me. She hasn't wanted to push, but as I confessed most things about Justin, Mom was pleased.

"He's a good man. I know he's a great friend to Ricky, and I believe if he makes you smile like you are, you should see where this goes."

That was last night.

Now, Mom's soft brown stare is again focused on me. "Have you changed your mind?" she asks again.

I shake my head.

"Devan, talk to me now. Whatever you're feeling, you need to face it before we're all seated at that table and Ricky says something to make you emotional."

"I'm not emotional," I say, wiping a tear with the back of my hand.

She reaches for my shoulders. "No, dear. You're not." Her smile grows. "What is making you not emotional?"

"I'm worried about Justin and Ricky."

Mom tilts her head.

"Justin said he's concerned if we don't work out that he'll lose both me and Ricky."

"Do you think you two won't work out?"

I sigh. "I don't know. Right now, I don't even want to think about that. But the friendship they share is important to both of them. I don't want to be the reason they lose it."

"I'm going to be blunt, Devan. You will change their friendship. It's simple. With you and Justin seeing one another, Justin will never again be only Ricky's friend. He'll also be yours."

Looking away from her gaze, I let her words sink in.

"Devan."

I look back up.

"Is Justin worth it?"

Without speaking, I nod.

"Does Justin think you're worth the risk?"

"I think he does. He's a little worried Ricky may take him out, right here in the kitchen."

Mom grins. "It's why I decided on chicken. I didn't want any steak knives at the ready."

"Do you think—?"

"No. I'm teasing you."

I let out a long breath. "We have your support, Justin and I?"

"You, Devan Marie, have my support. Your father and I are so proud of you, and that includes the decisions you've made. Why would I think that your ability to make choices has suddenly taken a turn? I don't. And the fact you're worried about Ricky and Justin's relationship shows what a truly loving woman you are."

"What about Dad?" I ask.

"He's coming to dinner prepared."

"You told him?"

Mom nods. "Your dad was surprised. The age difference caught him off guard, but the fact he knows Justin, and has known him... Well, Dad is willing to support you."

I didn't want her to tell Dad, but now that I know she has, I admit I'm relieved. "I guess that just leaves Ricky as the only one who will be blindsided."

We both look at the clock on the front of the microwave.

"What time is Justin getting here?" Mom asks.

"He said he'd text before he left his house." I pull my phone from the back pocket of my jean shorts and look at the screen. "No text."

"It's your decision." She pauses. "We can go ahead with the plan, or I can finish up the potatoes and fruit and you can go upstairs and have an adult conversation with your brother."

I lay my hand over my stomach. "I think I feel sick."

Mom doesn't speak.

"Fine," I say. Looking at the unfinished potatoes, I add, "just be sure to leave lumps."

Mom leans closer and kisses my forehead. "I love you. Rick does too. Remember that when he reacts. He's reacting to news about his baby sister."

"I'm not a baby."

"Remind him."

Taking a deep breath, I head toward the back staircase, the direction Ricky disappeared. With each step, I try to categorize the relationship the two of us share. With ten years' difference in our ages, we weren't exceptionally close when I was young. As Justin said, I was the tagalong little sister. Over the last few years, Ricky and I have grown closer. We talk more. He told me about Mom and Dad maybe selling the farm. I recall how proud he was at my graduation.

Two adults.

Yeah. We can be two adults.

As I near the bathroom we share, I hear the shower still running.

If I go back downstairs, I know I won't have the courage to come back up. Instead, I head into my bedroom and take another look at myself in the mirror. It's a June evening, and I'm dressed for the softball game, wearing jean shorts with a tear in one leg and ragged hems. They're short, but not too short. The orange tank top says Riverbend on the front. Marilyn and Jill will have on matching tops. They were made as a fundraiser for the team. If Riverbend has anything, it's pride in our local teams.

My light hair is still in the low ponytail I wore to the school earlier today. As I hear the water stop, I pull the hair tie from my hair, brush the length, and plait one long braid. By the time I'm done, I've heard the bathroom door open and Ricky's door close.

The phone in my back pocket vibrates. With a deep breath, I pull it out and read the screen.

"ON MY WAY."

Do you want to forget about this for a while?

That's the question I'm dying to text. The problem with doing so is that if Justin and I continue as we have been doing, this talk with Ricky will only get more difficult not less.

Two adults.

Ignoring the perspiration coating my skin and the erratic beating of my heart, I make my way to Ricky's bedroom door and knock.

"I'll be down in a minute."

"Ricky, it's Devan. Can we talk?"

The door opens. He's wearing a pair of basketball shorts. That's all. His bare chest and toned abs are on display. I can admit that he's good looking in a brother-type way. If he found someone, I'd be happy for him.

Two adults.

Ricky's stare is on me. Concern shows in lines beside his eyes. "What's the matter?"

"I wanted to talk with you before dinner."

He pushes the door open wider. "Is it something with Mom or Dad? Your new job?"

"No. It's…" I inhale. "I invited Justin to dinner." I lean against the doorjamb, taking in the clutter that is my brother. His bed is unmade. The clothes he wore while working today are half in and half out of a clothes basket. There are water bottles, a few pop cans, and God only knows what else on his bedside stand.

"Okay," he says, digging through a drawer of his dresser. Finally, he pulls his softball shirt from the depths. It's wrinkled, but at least it's clean. "Why?"

"We want to talk to you and Mom and Dad."

My brother's nose scrunches. "You and Justin want to talk to all of us. About what?"

Is it awful I want him to figure it out before I have to say it?

It is.

I need to say it.

I want a relationship with Justin. This is our first obstacle, and we both need to face it head-on. Clearing my throat, I say, "We're dating."

Ricky laughs as he pulls the orange shirt over his head. "Right. Is this a joke?"

"No." I shake my head. "It only became official last night, but it started the night of the hog roast."

My brother's expression goes blank. "The hog roast? The one at the Gordon farm? You weren't in town."

"I was. I came for my interview with Mr. Sams— Cory." I don't know what Justin said to Ricky about that night. "He didn't know who I was that night. And I didn't tell him."

Ricky shakes his head. "No. Justin wouldn't do this without talking to me, telling me."

"We didn't want to keep it from you. We were waiting to see if we both felt the same way."

"What way?" Ricky's voice is louder than before.

"We like one another."

"Shit, Devan. Tell me this is a poorly timed April fool's joke. It's fucking June."

"It's not," I say. "I like Justin. He likes me. We're adults. We're dating." As I finish speaking, we both turn to the sound of the screen door slamming.

"Come on in, Justin," my mom says on the first level.

"Ricky?" I question.

My brother pushes past me, determination filling his expression as he heads for the kitchen.

Chapter Twenty-One

Justin

As I enter the Dunns' home, I attempt to stop their screen door from slamming. The damn thing has done it for thirty years. I'm not sure why I think I can stop it now or why I care. Turning, I see Janet Dunn. "Hi," I say, as the door slams. "Sorry." My stomach rumbles at the delicious aroma filling this kitchen.

Janet waves her hand. "Come on in, Justin. That old door is better than any alarm system. If I didn't hear it slam ten times a day, I'd think my hearing would need checking." She comes closer to me.

My pulse speeds, and I'm pretty sure perspiration is forming on my brow.

"I'm glad you could come to dinner."

She's acting odd.

Weird.

She knows.

"Have you spoken with Devan?" I ask.

"I have. She's my daughter."

Inhaling, I debate about explaining my intentions—that they're good. I'd never do anything to hurt her daughter. Devan is amazing, and I want to spend time with her. When we're apart, she's all I think about. When we're together, I think of ways to make her happy. It's all new, but I promise I'll never intentionally hurt her.

Before I can get what would undoubtedly be another session of word-vomit to come forth, Mrs. Dunn speaks again. "You're a good man, Justin. Jack and I want nothing more than our children's happiness."

"I want her to be happy, too."

We both turn at the pounding of footsteps coming from the back stairs. Ricky's wingspan allows him to hold both side walls of the stairwell as he stops at the bottom. His eyes are on me, and there's no doubt in my mind he knows why I'm at dinner.

"The fuck?" my best friend growls.

"Ricky," Janet scolds.

I steady my voice. "I wanted to tell you."

Devan appears behind Ricky. If my goal is to make her happy, I can guess by the expression on her face that I'm failing.

"Outside," Ricky says.

"Really?" Devan yells.

Ricky barely gives her a look as he storms past me through the door, leaving us with a slam.

I turn to Devan and feign a smile. "It seems to be going well so far." She's sexy and sweet all rolled into one. A bra strap is barely showing from beneath her River-bend tank top. Her jean shorts accentuate her perfect ass without being too short. The white tennis shoes she's wearing fail at giving her extra height. Her soft brown eyes are stunning, and her hair is braided as it was yesterday.

Devan's scowl morphs to a smile as she comes toward me. Laying her hand on my arm, she makes eye contact. Oh fuck. She wants to kiss. Right here. In front of her mother.

Bite the bullet.

That's what I tell myself.

It's not like kissing Devan is a bad thing.

We both lean forward, our lips touching. The millisecond kiss was not one of our top ten, but that doesn't mean I don't return her smile. "Hi."

"Justin," Ricky yells from outside.

"I'm going to guess," I say, "that you told him."

Devan nods. "I told Mom last night. She told Dad. It didn't seem right for Ricky to be the only one who was caught off guard."

I completely understand. I also wish I would have been the one to do it. I turn from Devan to Janet. "If you'll excuse me." My smile ramps up. "Maybe one of you should get the nine and one dialed onto your phone to be ready."

"Dinner will be ready when you and Rick are," Janet says.

With a sigh and a nod, I push open the door, stuff my hands in my front pockets, and stand on the porch. Ricky is waiting, standing beside his truck, his arms crossed over his chest. When I'm close enough to speak at a normal tone, I say, "Go ahead and hit me."

"My sister?"

I nod.

"She's a kid."

"No, she isn't. You're the one who said that. Remember? We were on our way to her apartment, and you were talking about how she's grown up."

Ricky kicks the gravel by his bare feet. When he looks up, he asks, "The girl you mentioned, the one you met at the hog roast, the one you kept asking people about" — his expression saddens— "she was Devan?"

"She is Devan," I correct.

"No, you didn't describe my sister."

"I described the way I see her." I take a deep breath. "I didn't know she was the girl until we showed up at her apartment to help her move."

His gaze narrows. "The closed bedroom door."

"I'm the one who closed it."

Grunting, he looks down at the gravel. When he looks up, he says, "I'm remembering that time Cory and I had to pull you off Richards."

I nod.

This is not the same thing. Instead of trying to explain the differences, I sigh. "Go ahead. Give me your best shot. I won't hit you back."

"I'm not fucking hitting you. You're my friend. My best friend." He lowers his arms. "I don't know what to think." His expression turns as if he's eaten something sour. "Fuck, I don't want to think about you with her. Together. Dating..."

"Yes."

His grin quirks up on one side. "You haven't dated in a long time. Do you even remember how?"

A smile lifts my cheeks. "I'm not that fucking old."

He lifts his hand. "Don't tell me."

"Are we good?" I ask.

"No." His gaze meets mine. "We're not bad." He wraps his arm around my neck and pulls my head down, the way we used to do. "I'm not hitting you now, but I reserve the right to do it if you deserve it."

"Deal."

We turn as Jack's truck is approaching the garages.

"Does Dad know?" Ricky asks quietly.

"Devan said Janet told him." I stand tall, my hands clasped behind me, and wait as Jack Dunn steps out of his truck.

"Justin." He nods. "Ricky, I think dinner's waiting." And he walks past us.

When I let out the breath I am holding, Ricky laughs. "Seems like we're both going to hold onto that punch option for later." He turns and looks at me. "Where's your softball shirt?"

"In the wash."

Ricky laughs louder. "It was stuffed in your ball bag."

"No," I lie. It was in my bag. Even the bag is airing out. I eye Ricky up and down. "I just wanted it less wrinkled, so I wouldn't look all shitty like you."

"So that's how it's going to be. Making yourself look good for my sister?"

"Yeah," I say with a nod.

"Good. She deserves that much." He slaps my shoulder. "Let's eat."

Devan's smile is radiant as Ricky and I enter the kitchen. The seating chart from the other night has changed. Jack is still at one end and Ricky is at the other. This time, Janet is alone, and I'm seated beside Devan.

"Everything good?" Jack asks as he leans back and places a napkin on his lap.

My gaze goes to Devan's smile and back to Mr. Dunn. "Very good, sir."

Jack shakes his head. "Don't be getting all formal on us, Justin. My name's Jack, same as it was yesterday and the day before."

"Everything is very good, Jack."

Soon, everyone is picking up serving dishes filled with roasted chicken, mashed potatoes, green beans, and fruit, each person serving themselves and passing the dish to the next person. As it was with the chili, the meal is delicious. Even when Ricky complains about the potatoes having lumps, I'm too busy shoveling food in my mouth to notice. Watching Devan, I'm again noticing how she's not afraid to eat in front of me, and I know it's one of the things I'm starting to love about her.

Like about her.

Definitely like.

"I have cherry pie," Janet says as we start to slow the intake of dinner.

Shaking my head, I say, "I won't be able to run the bases if I eat any more."

"I can send a piece home with you. I picked it up today at Quintessential Treasures. Kandace is opening a section to fresh, home-baked items. It's supposed to be Thursday through Saturday, but when I stopped by this afternoon, she said she was already almost sold out. I had the choice of cherry or rhubarb."

I reply, "As long as Kandace didn't bake them, either one is probably good."

Everyone laughs.

Tonight, everyone pitches in clearing the table, the way it has always been at my house. Despite the rocky start, the Dunns make me feel comfortable, just like they always have, as if I'm a part of their family.

A quick look at the clock tells me I need to get moving for the game. My first stop is home, hoping Mom moved the shirt from the washer to the dryer.

"I'll walk you to your truck," Devan says, reaching for my hand.

After saying good night to her parents, the two of us

go outside, hand in hand. When we stop, Devan is abso-lutely beaming. Her smile takes my breath away, and the gleam in her chocolate eyes makes me not want to look away.

"I'm so happy," she says.

"Me too. I made it out without bodily injury."

Devan laughs. "I'll see you at the game."

"You could ride with me to the game."

"Marilyn is picking me up."

"I told my mom about us," I confess. "She said to tell you she's happy and would like to get to know you."

Devan opens her eyes wide. "This is really happening."

"It is. And I don't care how you get to the game. Just be prepared. I'm going to walk up those bleachers and kiss the most beautiful girl I know, in front of all of Riverbend."

"Why?"

"Because I can."

My answer seems to satisfy her.

"I'll see you tonight," she says, leaning toward me.

Cupping her cheek, I bring our lips together. We've had more passionate kisses, but this one says more than our earlier hello kiss did. It says that Devan Dunn is my girl. My woman. My lady. She's mine, and I don't mind if the whole damn world knows.

Chapter Twenty-Two

Devan

"Bye, I'm leaving," I yell to Mom and Dad before going outside.

Marilyn's car comes to a stop behind mine out by the garages. Before I get to her car, she and Jill both open their doors wide and jump out. Wearing their River-bend tank tops, they're both screaming, waving their arms in the air, and running in place. My cheeks warm as I get closer.

"Oh, she's blushing," Jill says.

"Tell us everything," Marilyn adds.

Tilting my head, I grin. "Tell you what? Oh, about my classroom. I've been working on it for days and you—"

"Shut up," Marilyn interrupts as she puts her fist on her hip. "Are you really officially dating Justin Sheers?"

I nod.

My quiet response earns me more screams.

"Does this have anything to do with the text message I received last night?" Jill asks.

"Yes. We had our first official date." I peer back at my house. "Could we maybe talk about it in the car on the way to the game?"

My two best friends open their eyes wide as they stare at one another and then at me. "This is going to be good," Jill says.

"Juicy good," Marilyn replies. She looks again at my house. "And your text said that your family knows?"

"I told Mom last night. She told Dad. Ricky found out today."

"And Justin is still alive?" Jill asks.

"It went better than I anticipated," I say truthfully. "Oh, and Justin said he told his mom."

Jill opens the door to the back seat. "You take shotgun, Devan. We want to hear every word you say."

Marilyn turns down the music as she backs up her car. Maneuvering a three-point turn, she heads out on the lane. "Where did you go on your date?"

"Empire Quarry."

"I thought that was blocked off," she says.

"I think it is. Justin knew a back way to get in." My smile grows. "It was beautiful. He packed a picnic."

"A picnic," they both scream and aww.

"It was super sweet," I say.

Jill wiggles her eyebrows. "Did you do more than eat your picnic?"

"Yes, we had wine. From Oliver."

Jill laughs. "He's pulling out all the local flair."

"Oh," Marilyn says, "We should plan your wedding shower for the winery. Remember how great Crystal's was?"

"Whoa," I say. "Jumping the gun. We're dating."

Marilyn slows her car and pulls to the side of the road. "We'll be in town in a few minutes. Tell us…"

"Tell you?" I say, playing dumb.

"Are you still a virgin?" Jill blurts out.

"Yes."

They both look sad.

"Jeez, we became official last night."

"I know," Marilyn says, "but he's older and I wanted stories like I read in romance novels about an older guy." She shakes her shoulders. "You know, being all instructional."

I don't say a word.

"Devan," Jill screams.

"We didn't go all the way."

"How far did you go?"

Their pressure is killing me. I let out a long breath. "It was amazing. I've never come so hard in my entire life."

Both of my friends have their eyes open wide.

"Justin asked me if I am a virgin."

"You told him?" Marilyn asks.

"No. I didn't answer him. He said he wants to go at my speed."

"What is your speed?" Jill asks.

My smile grows. "After last night, I'm thinking about the speed of light."

"Oh my God," Jill says, turning to Marilyn. "Our little girl is about to become a woman."

"Hey. I'm a woman. I have a real job and a college degree. I can vote and buy liquor..."

"I'm jealous," Marilyn says as she pulls her car back out onto the road. "Jill has Todd. Now you have Justin. I'm going to be alone forever."

"You're going to grad school," I remind her. "Remember, you don't have time for a guy."

Her lower lip protrudes in a pout.

"You can plan *my* bridal shower at Oliver," Jill says.

We all laugh.

"Let's go cheer on Riverbend," I say, "and be on the lookout for someone for Marilyn."

After a stop at the Tastee Freeze for large pops, we arrive at the ball field. With our cups in hand, Marilyn, Jill, and I climb the metal bleachers. They're beginning to fill with people we know from Riverbend. I say hi to Judy Sams, Cory's wife. She asks me a few questions about my class. I tell her how excited I am to teach science.

The Mitchell team is on the field, throwing the ball to one another. I look around the stands, noticing Chloe Reynolds and Kandace Richards seated just to our left.

Kandace is Justin's sister.

The soda pop churns in my stomach.

As more and more people arrive, I think about the last thing Justin said, about kissing me in the stands because he can.

Noise behind the stands grows louder.

Everyone stands and applauds as the Riverbend team runs onto the field. It doesn't take me any time at all to find Justin with his auburn hair and wide shoulders. The entire team is doing some weird chant before coming together in a group and yelling.

It's like the breaking apart of an atom as they scatter in different directions.

Mick Reynolds makes his way to his wife, Chloe.

Dax Richards makes his way to his wife, Kandace.

Marilyn reaches for my knee as Justin appears at the bottom of the stands. I sit very still, unsure if I'm ready for this major announcement, and also afraid he doesn't want to make it.

"Shit, shit..." Jill whispers.

Time slows as Justin climbs the steps in the middle of the bleachers. The night falls scarily quiet as his blue gaze finds mine and the tips of his lips curl upward. I'm caught in a time and space continuum, unable to move or speak as Justin comes closer.

Not acknowledging anyone else, Justin lays his hand on my knee. "I was informed that it's good luck to kiss your girl before a game."

I swallow.

He leans in, his penetrating stare on only me as his lips take mine. When he pulls away, his grin is panty melting. "There's no way we'll lose now." He smiles at my friends. "Jill and Marilyn. Nice to see you."

They reply.

It's all garble.

The fire scorching through my circulation is melting my mind to goo.

I'm overwhelmed with what he just did as he goes back down the bleachers.

Putting my head down, I whisper, "Is it my imagination or did everyone see that? Is everyone staring?"

"Not your imagination," Marilyn says as she lifts her hand and gives her best Queen Elizabeth wave.

"Holy shit," Jill says, "you were right. You're definitely official now."

The first inning remains scoreless. In the top of the inning, Mitchell loads the bases. Cory strikes the next batter out. Justin catches a line drive past second base. It is Dax Richards who catches the third out, leaping into the air near the fence. In the bottom of the first, Riverbend manages a double before getting three outs in a row. Justin never makes it up to bat.

As the teams change places for the second inning, Kandace Richards takes a seat in front of us. I've heard the rumor that she's expecting their second child. Without staring, it's hard to tell. Nevertheless, she's pretty. Her hair is the same color as her brother's, and her eyes are just as blue.

"You're Devan."

Even though I'm sure she knows who I am, I reply, "Yes, Devan Dunn and you're Kandace."

She smiles. "I am. I wanted to say hi."

"Hi." I try to make conversation. "My mom bought a cherry pie from your store today. It was delicious." Truthfully, I didn't eat any. I'm being polite.

"I didn't bake it. But I'm glad it was good. I was thinking that maybe you and Justin could come over to our house one day soon. I'd love to get to know the woman who can make my brother smile."

The last part of her statement makes my cheeks warm.

Kandace laughs. "It seems he makes you smile too. It's true, miracles do happen."

She seems genuinely happy for Justin, and even though we've unofficially met many times, I appreciate that she's reaching out to me. "Getting together would be fun," I say. "Justin adores Molly."

She nods. "Molly adores him too."

I look around for the little girl.

"She's not here," Kandace says. "The start time of the game was too late for her schedule. Mom is watching her at our house." She winks. "No rush, but Mom is great with grandchildren."

That makes me laugh. "That is a rush."

We turn to the field, seeing that the game has restarted.

Kandace pats my knee. "Good talking with you."

"You too," I say with a nod as Kandace goes back to her original seat.

"Damn, girl," Marilyn whispers. "Minus an announcement in the local paper, this is as official as it gets."

Mitchell finishes the inning without a score.

Justin is first batter in the bottom of the second. I'm clasping my hands so tightly, I'm pretty sure they've lost circulation. He said that kissing his girlfriend is supposed to be good luck.

If he doesn't get a hit, am I bad luck?

My stomach is in knots as the umpire calls two balls and one strike.

Tapping the bat against his shoe, Justin's blue gaze finds mine. He grins. I'm not sure if it really happened or I imagined it. My breath catches as the pitcher releases the ball.

Crack.

Everyone stands to their feet as the ball sails through the air. Justin is rounding second when the umpire yells, "It's out of here. Hooome ruuun." He stretches out the final two words.

Justin's pace slows as he rounds the final two bases to the clamorous applause of the home team crowd. The palms of my hands are red and sting from clapping. I hug Jill on one side and Marilyn on the other.

It's a defensive game. Riverbend pulls out the win with a 3 to 2 final score.

As we make our way down the bleachers, I have the

sensation of wading through uncharted waters. Usually, Jill, Marilyn, and I would either grab ice cream or call it a night. Because of Ricky, I know after the games many people head over to Decoy Ducks. I honestly don't know if that includes wives and girlfriends.

I spot Justin pushing against the crowd. He's searching, his lips pursed and his forehead furrowed. When his gaze lands on me, his handsome face magically morphs into a grin. Taking my hand, he tugs me from the masses to beneath the bleachers. His stare is like the simmering embers from a blazing fire. Without a word, he cups my cheek and pulls me close for a kiss. The heat within me grows, almost making me forget where we are.

Justin pulls back with a grin. "You did it. You're my good luck."

"*You* did it. The only home run of the night."

"Come with me to Decoy Ducks."

We both turn as Justin's name is being called by a few of his teammates. I can't help noticing Ricky. He's watching us and his expression is unreadable. I push up and kiss Justin's cheek. "I have a meeting early tomorrow morning at the school with the science department to discuss curriculum. Have fun with your friends."

"I'd rather have fun with you," he says, flashing his sexy smirk.

I tilt my head toward my brother. "I want you to myself. I also won't take you from the guys who have been your comfortable rut. We need to work on balance."

Justin nods. "Tomorrow night. Dinner."

"How fancy?"

"I'll wear a clean shirt."

"Oh, lucky me."

He gives me one more kiss and our hands slowly release one another.

"Six o'clock," he says.

"I'll be ready."

Chapter Twenty-Three

Justin

Cory sets a pitcher of beer on our table near the pool tables at Decoy Ducks. "Great game," he announces. His eyes land on me seated beside Ricky. "Hell of a lot better than I anticipated."

It's Ricky who speaks up. "You're all whispering like old ladies at a church social."

The entire table around me laughs. I know my teammates have been whispering about Devan and me.

Ricky refills glasses around the table, draining the new pitcher. With his glass in his hand, he stands. "The rumors are true."

My heart is slamming against my breastbone.

"My little sister Devan has decided to give this asshole a chance." He shrugs. "You are all my witnesses." Ricky looks at me. "If Justin doesn't treat Devan right, I'm going to need help hiding his body."

Glasses raise, clinking together as the discussion goes from the best way to transport a body to the best locations for hiding a body. The entire conversation would be entertaining if I wasn't the body they were trying to dispose of and if their ideas weren't so well thought-out.

The thing about living in rural America not far from major thoroughfares is that more than once, the land around Riverbend has been the location of said bodies. No one wants to find a partially eaten, decomposing corpse in the spring after the thaw. It's not a pretty sight.

That may be the reason my friends have such wide-ranging opinions.

"Plastic is a must," Galvin says. "Dexter was onto something."

"State park, deep in the woods."

"No, weigh him down in one of the quarries."

"I heard if you plant chili peppers, the cadaver dogs can't smell the body."

Ricky perks up. "We grow some great peppers."

"My grandma," Nick says, "mentioned endangered species. No one would cut down a whitebark pine to look for a body buried beneath."

"Is that why she had the Christmas tree farm?" Mick asks.

"What happened to your grandfather?"

As the group laughs and banters back and forth,

Cory sits to Ricky's side and leans forward. "Seriously, I'm glad you two are okay."

Ricky looks at me and shrugs. "We are now, but I know I've got a great crew here. They'll have my back."

Cory's focus is on me. "I thought about what you said. Devan is an adult. The parents of her students will need to see her that way."

"It's Riverbend," Ricky says. "It will take some time, but they'll come around."

"Seriously," I say, proud of my girl, "check out her classroom. She's been working her ass off."

"You've seen it?" Ricky asks.

"Yeah. Go look at it. She's proud of all the work she's done."

Ricky stands. "Next pitcher is on me." He laughs. "No, it's on Justin."

The table cheers.

Once Ricky is gone, I turn to Cory. "I don't want to be a negative influence on Devan. I'd never do that."

"No," he sighs. "You're not. I was worried you were..." He grins and shakes his head. "It doesn't matter. I was wrong, and now the entire fucking county knows about the two of you."

"I'm pretty sure it's made national news by now."

When I climb into bed, my final thoughts for the day are of Devan. Lying there, I realize that as much as I like her, I have been worried about Ricky and his parents. Yesterday, that concern spread to Cory and others in Riverbend. Tonight, the weight is off my shoulders.

The entire world knows that Devan Dunn is my girl.

As I drift off to sleep, I'm not thinking about what-ifs.

I'm thinking about now-whats.

What can I do or say to convince Devan she's meant for me and I'm for her?

After breakfast at the diner, I head back to the farm. Not every day is spent in the sun, dirt, and fresh air. Days like today are spent in Dad's office working on profit and loss, budgets, making allowances for the increased price of seed and fertilizer. Even though I've modernized our books, I spend a lot of time flipping through old paper spreadsheets.

You can learn from the past. If you don't, you'll suffer the same setbacks.

I'm on my fourth cup of coffee when Dad steps in.

"What is it?" I ask, seeing his expression.

"Jack just called. That developer upped his offer."

"Fuck," I growl, leaning back in the worn office chair. "We can't compete."

Dad takes the seat on the other side of his own desk. "I met with Jeffrey Murphy, the lawyer."

"Yeah, I know who Jeffrey Murphy is. Why not talk to Dax?" He's an attorney too.

"I wanted a less biased opinion."

"And what did he say?" I ask.

"He said if we mortgage our land, with today's prices, we can buy the Dunns' farm, all of it."

"All of it? You mean the house and barns too?"

Dad nods. "All of it."

I sit forward. "I didn't know Jack and Janet wanted to sell the whole thing. What about Ricky and Devan?"

"I know this is awkward," Dad says.

Pushing the chair back, I run my hand through my hair. "It's not awkward, Dad. I just..." I sigh. "I don't want that developer tearing their property into pieces. We don't need the traffic. Hell, the development itself—building the infrastructure—will take a few years at least. And I was talking to Mick Reynolds the other day. His construction firm was hired to do repairs on some of those new houses south of town. The damn surveyors didn't take into consideration the increase in impervious surfaces and runoff. The heavy rains last spring. A shit-ton of those houses had flooded basements."

"The Dunns?"

"I want them to get the most they can for their property." I meet my dad's gaze. "Not by mortgaging our land."

"It's the smartest move, son. With their land, our acreage doubles. Our crops double."

"So do our expenses. So do our possibilities for failure. A damn seed-corn maggot infestation and we're fucked."

"Have you talked to Ricky about it?"

"Not recently."

"Devan?"

I smirk. "You know?"

"Your mom and I don't keep secrets. That's my advice for you and Devan."

"Right. Tonight, at dinner I'll compliment how great she looks and segue into what she wants to happen to her family's land. I know, I'll bring it up right before asking how her meeting went with the science department."

"There are some big decisions that will need to be made. I'm sorry if the timing doesn't work for the two of you. That's life."

"I'd rather keep life out of our bubble at the moment."

"No one can fault you for that." Dad stands. "You know, your grandfather put his faith in me to keep this farm going. I was a little older than you when he passed away. It was a scary time. Do you know who kept me sane through it all?"

"Me," I say with a grin.

"Hell no. You were into everything, and Kandace was only a baby."

"You're going to say Mom."

Dad nods. "Mr. Murphy thinks we need to make a counteroffer."

"Dax?"

"He agrees."

"Where the hell have I been in all these discussions?"

"I'd say where you were, but you know."

Chapter Twenty-Four

Devan

"I like the dress," Marilyn says, lying on my bed.

I stand before my full-length mirror and pitch right and left. The long skirt flows near my ankles where I'm wearing gold sandals with rhinestones. This dress is light green and unlike the one the other night, it has a more complete bodice, allowing me to wear a bra. "He didn't say how to dress."

Jill's eyebrows dance. "Because he wants you undressed."

"He said dinner," I remind my friends.

Jill sits straight. "Have I told you about the time Todd said we were going to dinner, but he didn't tell me that he was the one who would be eating."

"Yes," Marilyn and I say in unison.

"Oh." She pouts. "Sorry, with all this Justin talk, I'm missing Todd."

"When is he getting back from that conference in Atlanta?" Marilyn asks.

"Sunday night." Jill's smile widens. "I'm going to surprise him at his apartment." She gestures wide with her hands. "I have it all planned out."

"Okay," I say. "If this was part of your big plan, would you wear this dress" —I gesture to the one I have on— "or this one" —I point to one shorter and more casual— "or just go with capris?"

"My plan includes a bubble bath and no clothes."

I shake my head. "You're no help."

"I know," Marilyn says. "Wear the one you have on. It fits great and you're beautiful."

I turn again to the mirror and lift my long hair. I have it all down and flowing. It's warm on my neck. "I don't know. It feels a little stuffy."

"That's my plan," Marilyn says. "Don't wear panties."

My eyes open wide. "What?"

Jill bounces on the side of the bed. "Oh my God, she's right." Jill lifts her hand to me. "I mean, look at you. You're the proper schoolteacher, but just before the waitress brings your meal, casually lean close and whisper, 'I forgot to put on panties.'"

I shake my head. Without trying, I imagine the scene. "I can't do that."

"You've never done that. It's not that you *can't* do it," Marilyn says. "Justin wants to know your speed."

Jill chimes in. "Nothing says light speed ahead like going commando."

"Where is he taking you?" Marilyn asks.

"I don't know."

"You need to ask more questions."

"I like the surprise."

Marilyn's eyes widen. "You like surprises. I bet he does too."

My phone lying on the bed between my two friends lights up. As it does, I hear my mom's voice from downstairs.

"Devan, Justin is here."

With two sets of eyes on me, I sense the drop in temperature of the room. No, it's rising—exponentially —as my cheeks flush. "Seriously?"

"Yes," they both say.

Hiking the skirt of the dress, I snag the waistband of my panties, drag them down my legs, and step out of them. "There." The bikini-cut white panties with lace trim lands on the floor.

Jill and Marilyn clap.

"We want details," Jill says. "Remember, with Todd out of town, I'm living vicariously through you."

"Oh God." I feel faint as I consider what I just did.

My friends scurry from the bed. "Snap out of it."

"Should we splash water on her?"

"No," I say. "Mascara."

It's not that I wear a lot of makeup—just a little mascara, eyeliner, and pink stain on my lips.

"Devan," Mom calls again.

"If he breaks up with me, you're both fired as best friends."

Jill has her arms crossed over her chest. "He most definitely won't break up with you."

Taking a deep breath, I open my bedroom door. Before stepping into the hallway, I look back. "Throw those in the laundry. I don't want Mom to wonder."

They both laugh.

"And stay up here."

"You're no fun," Jill says.

Marilyn elbows her. "She will be later tonight."

Shaking my head, I walk down the hallway, ultra-alert of the airflow beneath the skirt of my dress. As I descend the stairs, the skirt fluffs. I push away images of the iconic Marilyn Monroe picture. I'm about to turn around and gather my panties when I see Justin at the bottom of the stairs.

His mesmerizing blue stare is on me as his cheeks rise and his lips curl into a smile. A trimmed line of facial hair frames his chiseled jaw. As my focus moves lower, I wonder if someone told him the color of my dress because his untucked button-up shirt is a shade darker. He has his sleeves rolled up to near his elbows, and his tan muscled forearms are visible. My focus moves over his jean-clad legs. His cloth loafers make me grin. I've never seen him wearing anything but boots or tennis shoes.

"Hi," I say with a smile, my nipples beading from the intensity of his stare. Once on the kitchen floor, I spin around, a full circle. "I hope this is all right. You didn't tell me where we are going."

"All right? Devan, you're gorgeous." He takes a step closer, and I'm immersed in an intoxicating cloud of fresh, clean scent mixed with a little spice of cologne. His large hand reaches for mine as we move closer, our lips brushing one another's.

It's then that the rest of the room comes into focus, and I see that we're alone. "My mom must trust you. She's not standing watch."

Justin smirks and lowers his voice. "She wouldn't trust me if she could read my thoughts right now."

The rumble of his voice and provocation in his words has my core twisting. Breathing deeply, I again ask, "Where are we going?"

"I happen to know the chef at Bynard's."

Bynard's.

My expression no doubt shows my excitement. At the same time, I'm worried I'm not dressed formal enough. Bynard's is a five-star restaurant on Lake Monroe. "It's prime season. How did you get reservations?"

Justin's eyes open wide. "Shit, do we need reservations?"

I laugh. "It's okay. We can go someplace else."

He offers me his bent arm. "We're going to Bynard's.

As I said, I have a connection and we have a reservation for seven thirty."

Wow.

I take a step back. "Are you sure I'm dressed okay?"

"If you ask me, you're overdressed."

Heat flares in my cheeks at my secret.

Once we're both in the truck, Justin leans closer, taking my breath as he kisses me deeper than he did in the kitchen. For a moment in time, our tongues slide over one another's. When he pulls back, his grin is spectacular. "I would have never been able to drive all the way to Bloomington if I didn't do that first." He starts the truck, and we begin our journey.

Along the way we talk about our day. I tell him about the big science department meeting. There are a few proposed adjustments in curriculum that we all needed to know and understand. "It's so weird to never have taught a class and be the one to make major changes."

"Do you feel good about the changes?"

I shrug. "It isn't anything like things you hear on the news. It's pretty basic stuff, like having my lesson plans ready before school starts. There's an internal review board. That way if anyone complains that I'm teaching the anatomy of an arachnid, the team has a ready response."

"Oh, arachnid anatomy," he says. "I can see how controversial that could be."

"You have no idea. In some species, their different

appendages can grow large enough to take on the appearance of an extra leg."

Justin laughs. "I didn't know that."

"Explaining that to seventh-grade boys..."

He lifts his hand. "Oh, stop. I see the problem already."

"Yep. The subject came up when I was student teaching and thankfully, the teacher was able to jump in. The scary thing is that now I'll be the teacher."

Justin's hand lands on my dress-covered thigh before his blue stare meets mine. "I have faith in you."

"How was your day?"

"Nothing as exciting as leg-sized appendages."

"I'm glad to hear that." I'm a terrible judge, but what I felt the other night and before at my apartment was large, but isn't exactly going to be mistaken for a third leg.

Justin's expression sobers.

"Is something wrong?"

He swallows, his Adam's apple bobbing in the V of his open shirt collar. "Fuck. I didn't want to talk about it tonight. I want tonight to be about us."

"Is it bad? Is there a problem? With us?" I ask.

"No," he answers quickly as the light mood of our talk slips away.

Instead of asking, I wait.

"I found out today," Justin says, "the developer offered your dad more money for the farm."

"Oh."

I suppose that should make me happy. I mean, my parents deserve to benefit from their years of hard work. The thing is that now that I'm back, I don't want them to sell.

"What are you thinking?" Justin asks.

Looking down at his hand still on my leg, I try to come up with words. "I want my parents to reap the benefit from all their hard work."

Justin nods.

"I also don't like change. I thought I did. I thought I wanted a different life than Riverbend. I don't regret leaving for college. Now that I'm back, I realize how much I love this place. I don't want to see it change. I don't want it to turn into every other town."

He squeezes my leg. "Dad has come up with a way for us to buy your farm."

"If the developer is offering more," I say, thinking aloud, "then that means you'd need to pay more."

Justin nods again.

"When do you need to decide? Does my dad know you're interested?"

"Jack knows. We've talked."

"Before we started dating?"

"Yeah." He grins. "You and I are an extra wrinkle."

"A wrinkle?"

"I'm stuck in the middle. Of course, I would like us to get the land at the lowest price, but I don't want to shortchange your parents." He smiles my direction. "I'd like to stay in their good graces."

"Don't take on more than you can handle or spend more than you can afford because of me."

"Devan, it's happening so fast that I can't keep up. However, since walking into your apartment and seeing you standing there, your hair all piled on your head. Your Ball State t-shirt...everything I do is because of you."

Chapter Twenty-Five

Justin

I owe Galvin big time for this favor. I hadn't thought of Bynard's until sometime this afternoon. For a Friday night in prime summer, getting a seat at the bar would be iffy. A reservation is impossible.

Not impossible.

Galvin is part owner and their head chef. Not a bad accomplishment for a guy who isn't yet thirty-three years of age. We razzed him in high school when he took cooking classes at the nearby career institute. It's a place open to multiple school districts that offers classes specializing in anything from vet tech, to landscaping, to culinary arts. They even have a restaurant.

Even though we teased Galvin, he knew his passion.

And for the record, just because the guy cooks, it doesn't mean he couldn't play football and softball with the best of us. While his parents don't have a lot, they wanted to help him. One summer he went to a cooking camp. Honestly, I don't remember what it was called, only that he barely lived it down. Turned out, the camp was a magnet camp for top culinary schools in the country. Galvin was offered a full scholarship to The Culinary Institute of America. Our friend spent four years in New York. Not only did he study, but he also had two internships at top New York City restaurants.

Lucky for those of us back in Indiana, he decided to come back home. His talents were sought after by bigger restaurants in Indianapolis and Evansville. The couple who opened Bynard's about six years ago knew Galvin when he was in New York.

The fucker is now part owner and head chef.

He is one of my friends who hasn't yet found the love of his life in the form of a human. He found it early on in his quest for a career. Let's just say, we don't razz him anymore.

With Devan on my arm, I approach the hostess stand.

"Reservations?" the hostess asks skeptically.

"Yes, two for Sheers."

Peering through her rhinestone-studded readers, the woman scans her tablet until her scowl morphs to a smile. "Yes." She reaches for menus and takes a step away from the stand. "You have one of our nicest tables, Mr. and Mrs. Sheers. We hope you enjoy your dinner. Please follow me."

Devan holds tight to my arm as we are led through a maze of tables, then through large glass doors to a patio. Strings of lights are overhead. The hostess takes us to a table for two near the railing of the patio. Lake Monroe is a reflection of the colorful clouds, our picturesque view as the sky overhead darkens. Before I can do it, the hostess pulls out a chair for Devan. By the time she unfolds our napkins and places them on our laps, I'm over the VIP attention.

When she finally walks away, my agitation disappears into Devan's laughter. "She was something else."

"If I ever forget how to place my own napkin, I know where to come."

My girl looks all around. "Justin, this is amazing." Her gaze comes back to me, and her forehead furrows.

"Talk to me."

"Who did you plan to bring here?"

"What? You."

She shakes her head. "I remember prom. We tried to get reservations, and they were booked months in advance. Since we became official two days ago..."

My cheeks rise. "You, Devan Dunn. I've been secretly stalking you for months."

I love how easily she blushes.

Reaching across the table, I lay my hand palm up. Slowly, she places her hand in mine. "The chef, who is also one of the owners, is one of my best friends. I called him today."

"Today," she says in amazement.

"This was planned only for you."

We've opened a bottle of wine, and we're sharing a plate of calamari. We've ordered our meals but asked for the waiter to take his time. The sky overhead is dark and beyond the stringed lights, other lights reflect on the reservoir's mirror-like surface.

"Did you hear what the hostess called us when she brought us back to the table?" I ask.

Devan nods with a grin. "Mr. and Mrs."

"I never thought there would be a Mrs. Sheers. I mean, other than my mom."

"Now?"

"For the first time, I see the possibility." I shake my head. "I'm not rushing you, Devan. I'm just over-whelmed...and you should know it's because of you." I lower my voice. "You decide the speed. I'll wait as long as you want."

Pink intensifies on her cheeks as Devan looks down. When her gaze meets mine, there's a spark simmering in her light brown orbs. "I have a secret."

"You do?"

She nods.

"Are you going to make me guess?"

"No. I wasn't planning on telling you until later in our dinner..." Her words come faster. "Well, if I told you at all. That is part of the debate. I'm not sure if I should, but now I've started and..."

Again, I reach across the table. "Whatever has you this nervous can wait if you want."

Devan covers my hand with hers. Her voice is so soft I strain to hear. And when I do, I wonder if I heard her correctly. "Excuse me," I say.

Her neck and face are now the color of a fire engine. "You heard me."

Shit, my dick is growing. "Tell me again."

"I'm not wearing panties."

Lifting my hand, I call, "Check please."

"No," Devan says with a giggle. "You brought me to the best restaurant in the state. I want my filet."

"Nope, sorry. We're leaving."

Her embarrassment fades into humor as she takes a drink of her water.

"Sir," our waiter says, appearing from nowhere. "Is there a problem?"

"Yes."

"No," Devan corrects. "We're great."

I nod. "We're great, but the kitchen can hurry with our order."

"Yes, sir."

"I may have to take mine to go," I say after he leaves. "I can't think of anything else other than what you just said." I look around. "On second thought, we'll be here all night. I'm afraid without a moving tote, I may never be able to leave this chair."

Devan lifts her wine glass. "To less-erotic thoughts."

Erotic.

We clink our glasses. "You're killing me."

"I'd rather have you around for a long time."

Somehow, I manage to eat my meal, and Devan does the same. When the waiter asks if we'd like dessert, I'm not even polite enough to ask Devan if she does. My answer is that I do, but what I want isn't served on the menu. I don't say that. I simply say no and ask for the check.

Gripping Devan's hand, I take her out into the parking lot. As I open my truck, I'm struck with the reality that we are two adults who live with our parents. Half of Riverbend may have lost their V card in the Gordons' barn, but that was when they were teenagers.

Devan Dunn isn't a teenager.

I don't know the status of her V card; however, I know what she is or isn't wearing under her dress. Now I'm wondering where we could go. Once I'm behind the wheel, I let out a long breath and lay my head against the seat. "For the first time in years, I'm upset I don't have my own place."

She reaches for me. "I don't care where we go. I want to be with you."

With me.

"That question I had…"

Devan grins. "Get me alone." She looks around. "Not in a parking lot, and we can talk about it. If talking is what you want to do."

The obvious answer is also not the best. Nevertheless, I can't come up with any other options.

When I pull up to a hotel from a large chain, Devan's

eyes open too wide. "Justin, I-I need to go home tonight. My parents..."

"I'm not pressuring you. I just want to be alone where we can't be interrupted. Fuck. We can only talk if you want." I reach for her hand. "Trust me?"

"I do."

Devan stands to my side as I pay for a room. This is new territory for me. I've never done something like this. Yes, I've had sex, but it was in the truck or barn or out under the stars. Or it was in the girl's bedroom, but checking into a hotel room with a beautiful woman at my side and no luggage—that's new.

She's quiet as we ride the elevator to the seventh floor.

"I'm not wearing panties." Her words are on a repeat track in my head. It takes all my willpower to not give that more thought. I could think about it less if she wasn't so damn close, the warmth of her body leaning against my arm.

Following the numbered signs, we find room 715.

The card makes the lock turn green. Twisting the handle, I open the door.

The room is a standard-fare hotel room. A closet, bathroom, and bedroom.

A king-sized bed.

"Are you all right?" I ask as she follows me into the room.

"I trust you."

Good. I'm not sure I can trust myself.

Chapter Twenty-Six

Devan

Justin shakes his head. "We can have a seat at that crappy round table and talk all night long if that's what you want."

I scan the room.

The table is pretty crappy. I mean, it's a decent chain, but not exactly five-star. For a moment, I consider hiding in the bathroom, but as my mind takes me to the next move, I don't have one.

Inhaling, I decide to face his dick question head-on. Putting my arms around his shoulders, I ask, "Did you mean it when you said you wouldn't care if I've been with anyone else?"

His jaw is rigid as he nods.

"You're not very believable."

Letting out a breath, Justin drops his forehead to

mine, his arms encircling me, his hands in the small of my back. "I'm lying," he admits. "I would care, but I wouldn't think less of you if that's what you're asking. Fuck, I know you're an adult. I've spent the last few days saying that to Ricky and Cory, and...fuck...everyone." He inhales, his wide chest pushing against my breasts. "I don't know what our future holds, Devan. I know without a doubt I want to be the last man you're ever with. That's what matters to me."

"And me to be the last woman?"

He nods. "I wake up wondering why you're even giving me a chance. I wanted to take you someplace tonight to show you how much I care about you. How proud I am to have you beside me. Last night, it felt like the entire town was watching me walk up to you in the bleachers. I felt a hundred sets of eyes on me. And with each step, something inside me grew. By the time I reached the top, I wanted to do more than gently kiss your lips. You do something to me, something basic or... shit...some caveman thing. You never have to explain what you did before me as long as you let me be the only one with you from now forward."

"That almost sounds like a proposal."

"It is. Not a marriage proposal. When that day happens, if it does, you won't be wondering if I really asked you to marry me. You'll know. This is a proposal to continue our exclusive seeing of one another. Dating or whatever it's called these days."

I nod.

"I need to warn you about something," he says.

I take a step back. "What?"

"Making announcements like you did tonight about your lack of panties will definitely have consequences."

My cheeks rise. "Oh, I like consequences." Tilting my head, I ask, "Will I like them?"

"It's my goal for you to like them a lot." Justin walks all the way around me. "The other night, you let me play with your amazing tits. Did you like that?"

Shit.

My nipples bead without him touching me.

"Devan?"

"I liked it," I say softly.

"My finger had the pleasure of your perfect pussy. Do you remember?"

Nodding, I smile. "I remember."

"Did you like that?"

"I think that was obvious."

"You mean by the way you came on my hand."

Inhaling, I feel the return of the fire to my cheeks. "Yes, that's what I mean."

Reaching for the buttons that run down the front of my dress, Justin undoes the top one. "There's something I'd like you to do for me." Gathering my hair, he gently lays it behind my shoulder. His lips pepper my sensitive skin behind my ear. "Will you do it for me?"

I'm pretty sure he could ask me to rob a bank and as the fire within me builds, I'd say yes.

I reach out to his arm, holding his shoulders, to keep

from falling. The sensation of his kisses and the rumbling of his voice wash through me in waves with the vigor of a rushing rapids. "Do what?" I manage to articulate.

He undoes another button and another.

"I need you to be one hundred percent honest with me."

My eyes open. That isn't what I was expecting. "I am honest."

His penetrating gaze is on me as his fingers continue with the buttons. "Tell me what you like and what you don't like. I want to make you feel good. I want you to get so worn out from feeling good that you can barely move." Another button.

My dress is agape to my waist.

He pushes the dress from my shoulders, and the green material flutters to the floor, creating a circle around my sandals. Justin's eyes open wide, the blue overpowered by the dilation of his pupils. His breaths come faster as he scans my exposed core.

Without instructions, I reach back and unlatch my bra. Soon it is lying on the carpeting with my dress.

"You're beyond stunning, Devan." His ghostly touch flits over my flesh as he again makes a complete circle, scanning me from my sandals to my hair, his gaze lingering in between. "Come here," he says. His baritone command isn't demanding, yet I have no thoughts of disobeying.

Justin reaches for the covers on the bed and flings them back. Toss pillows fly as the blanket and bedspread land on the floor. The large bed is only covered with pristine white sheets. He offers me his hand as he asks, "Did you like what we did the other night?"

My circulation heats with the concoction of memories and anticipation. "You know I did."

"I gave you other options. Do you remember?"

Biting my lip, I nod.

"Say them to me."

When I try to hide my face behind my hands, Justin grasps my wrists, pulling them away.

"I'm staring at you right now, Devan. You're perfect in every way. Never be embarrassed about us; be bold."

"I never have," I say.

"Never been bold? You can do it."

"No." I inhale. "I've never done..."

His eyes open wide. "What have you never done?"

Despite the fact I think this will change everything, I confess. Each phrase coming faster than the last. "Much of anything. Once I let this guy at Ball State do what you did, but..." I shake my head. "It wasn't. I didn't. He was all..." I scrunch my nose. "It was only awkward. Not like what others talk about...not like the other night. I figured I was defective or something."

"Fuck that. You're not defective."

"Dry hump," I say, remembering his options. "Or your tongue."

"Have you done either of those?"

"Dry hump, same result."

"No man has ever had his tongue in your pussy?"

I shake my head.

"Cock?"

"No, Justin," I say in frustration, taking a step away and scanning the floor for my dress. "You're making fun of me. You think I'm a kid now." With tears burning my eyes, I turn on him, my voice raising. "See, it was a double-edged question. There's no right answer—"

His lips crash down on mine as one hand grasps the back of my neck and his other arm snakes around my waist, pulling me to him. My thoughts and words fade in the intense flames of his desire. As his tongue mingles with mine and his lips take command, my entire body melds against his. The hard planes of his chest. The strength in his arms. And yes, his trapped erection beneath his jeans.

My lips gape as he pulls my hair, yanking my head back.

The pain is momentary. It's the scorching fire in his eyes that I feel.

"Devan, you're fucking right. There is no right answer. There was no wrong answer either, but damn it, you're not defective. I want to spend forever showing you that if you'll let me."

The relief is instantaneous. "You don't want to break up?"

"No. Why the hell would I want that?"

I remember what he said about me being bold. Keeping my gaze focused on him, I do what he did to me, unbuttoning his shirt. With each button, I kiss his hard chest. Fine auburn hair tickles my lips as I move lower. Button. Kiss. Button. Lick.

"Fuck," he growls.

I stop to tease his nipples, licking and nipping.

"Jesus, Devan."

Smiling, I look up through veiled lashes. "You told me to be bold. I never have, but I like it." I reach for the buckle of his belt.

Justin shakes his head. "I like you bold, but, baby, tonight, I'm in charge."

Something within me tightens, my core twists, and I'm hyperaware of everything.

The aroma of his cologne.

The hum of the air conditioner.

Justin's radiating warmth.

The deep timbre of his voice. "Up on the bed. Take off your sandals."

Doing as he said, I bend down and slip my feet from the sandals. Next, I scoot to the headboard where I watch him kick off his shoes, unfasten his belt, and remove his blue jeans.

Lord almighty.

Justin isn't going commando, but what he has under his boxer briefs is hardly hidden.

"Um," I say, my focus on his erection.

With a grin, he climbs onto the bed and before I know it, tugs my ankles until I'm staring up at the ceiling.

"What?"

The sensation of his lips on my inner thighs is like the

zap of electricity. No, lightning in a summer sky. I try to move, but his fierce grip of my knees has them spread apart, exposing my core.

"Justin."

"I'm not pushing," he says, his kisses going higher.

My left inner thigh.

My right inner thigh.

My thoughts scramble as his mouth attacks my core with the same voracity as when he hungrily kissed my lips. Grasping for the sheets, I hope they will keep me earthbound because I don't want to be anywhere else.

Each lick, suck, and nip winds my insides tighter. While he has one hand on my stomach, holding me in place, it is as if his touch is everywhere. He hasn't touched my breasts, yet my nipples are painfully hard.

I arch my back as he sucks my clit.

"Please," I pant.

More kisses to my thighs.

"Do you want me to stop?"

Stop.

"No, I'm so tight. I'm almost there," I say, being brutally honest.

My legs bend with my knees near my hips as Justin buries his face in my core. I've heard stories—mostly from Jill. I've also read stories, but those are fantasy.

What he's doing...

This is real.

Holy shit.

I buck my hips and call out his name as I come undone.

My orgasm isn't a quick fall from a ledge into the depths of a quarry. It's a rumbling locomotive, barreling through the countryside, out of control, sparks from the wheels igniting brush, flames and ash smoldering in its wake.

Earthshaking and draining.

My core convulses as his tongue continues lapping my essence. The erratic rhythm of my heart pounds in my ears. I pant to fill my lungs with air.

Justin's kisses move higher. My mound. My pelvis. My stomach. He lingers at my breasts until his handsome face is inches from mine. "Not defective."

A smile curls my lips. "I'm thinking maybe I wasn't the problem."

"You're definitely not the problem, Devan. Are we done?"

"Do you have condoms?" I ask.

He nods. "I'm not going to use them."

"Why?"

"Because I'm not going to fuck you tonight." He kisses my nose.

What?

"You don't want to?"

He shakes his head. "I want to. I also like that I get to be your first. It will be special." He looks around. "Not in some random hotel."

"With a crappy table," I say with a giggle.

"Are we done?"

My eyes open wide. "I don't know what else there is."

Justin rolls to his back and simultaneously pulls me over him. "Option three."

"Dry humping?"

"I doubt it will be dry, but it won't be intercourse."

Chapter Twenty-Seven

Justin

The wonder in Devan's expression is magical. "I've never..." Her words of uncertainty fade into the sounds around us.

Reaching up, I cup her cheek, staring into her milk-chocolate eyes. Without words, I want her to know she's the one in control. I took it, but I'm giving it back. She has me so damn gobsmacked that I'd gladly go wherever she leads. As she leans into my touch, I say, "I trust you."

Nodding, her smile returns. Moving her knees to the side of my hips, Devan sits upward. Tentative, she seems unsure if she can lower her weight, bringing her pussy to my erection.

"I won't break."

Placing her hands on my shoulders, Devan wiggles her ass. Her perfect tits bounce as her expression becomes a kaleidoscope. Each thought and each feeling are on full display. There's nothing defective or artificial about my girl. She's genuine in everything she does.

Devan settles over me.

I left her pussy warm, wet, and I expect, sensitive.

Her lips move as moans and whimpers fill the air.

Shit, as she grinds her core over my erection, I see fucking lights.

Fireworks.

I want to slow time, to let this last for the rest of the night. At the same time, I long to reach for her hips, push her down harder and move her over me. If I were alone in another cold shower, I would be much less gentle.

"Oh, I feel you..." Her voice is full of wonder while dripping with desire. "Yes...right there."

Moving my hands to behind my head, I stare up at her. My girl is a vision as she navigates this new road. Her heat penetrates my boxers as my cock grows impossibly harder.

I arch my back as the pressure within me builds.

Devan slows. Her eyes are open wide. "Am I...Is this right?"

"You're killing me in the best of ways." When she doesn't respond, I smile. "Keep going, Devan. Show me what feels good."

"I thought it was to make you feel good."

"Do you not like it?"

"I do," she answers quickly. "Do you?"

Moving one of my hands, I take her wrist and lead

her hand to my erection. "Tell me. Do you think I like it?"

Devan nods with a grin. "I'm doing that? Because of me?"

"One hundred percent because of you."

"Okay." She takes a deep breath.

Again, I clasp my hands behind my head. The slow grind continues to build. Devan leans in, her breasts close to my chest as she finds her own sweet spot. With her eyes closed, her movements come faster.

Fuck.

I won't last much longer.

Her fingernails dig into my shoulders as her noises and movements speed. I can't help the way my hips push against her, yet she isn't shying away.

"Yes," she screams.

She says it again.

Giving up any resistance, I concentrate on her pussy over my cock. "Yes."

I can't stop myself from reaching for her thighs as I buck against her. "Fuuuckkk," I elongate the word as I come. Holding her in place, I close my eyes, my cock throbbing between us as warm wetness squirts onto my stomach and hers.

When I open my eyes, I'm not sure what I'll see.

A vision.

That's what I see.

Devan's smile is stunning.

"I did it," she says. "You came."

"So did you."

She nods.

"Fuck, Devan. I could have come the minute you got on top of me. I lasted as long as I could."

She buries her face in my shoulder.

When I realize what is happening, that she's crying, I panic. Grasping her shoulders, I roll us until we're reversed and I'm over her. "What's the matter? I didn't hurt you?" My questions come faster. "Did I...? Fuck, if you weren't ready—"

Devan lays her finger on my lips. "Nothing is wrong. I was so afraid that I couldn't...you wouldn't... I was petrified that you'd think I didn't know what I was doing, or I was bad at it."

I frame her cheeks with my palms. "Never think that." I grin. "You're a natural."

"I have a good instructor."

"You don't need one, but if the position is open, I'll apply."

"You already have the job," she says.

I kiss her nose again. "I would love to spend the night with you in my arms."

Devan sighs. "I need to be home."

Looking at my watch, I see it's almost midnight. "I sure as fuck hope you don't have a curfew."

She rolls, looking at the clock. "No, but we should go." Sitting up, she reaches for the sheet and wipes her stomach.

"You've been marked," I say with a smirk.

"That's so barbaric."

"Oh, sorry. It won't happen again."

Leaning closer, her lips come to mine. "I hope it does."

We both take a minute to clean ourselves. By the time we're ready to check out, we appear mostly normal. Devan's lips are redder and puffier than when we arrived. I smell her sweet essence on my face and my boxer briefs are headed to the laundry when I get home.

"I can turn in the key if you want to wait," I offer.

Devan shakes her head, her long hair swaying. "No, Justin. I'm not ashamed of anything we just did. Two adults."

"Two adults who need a private place of their own," I say.

"There's no rush. I'm not going anywhere."

Hugging her to my side, I kiss the top of her head. "I'm afraid that ship sailed. I'm not letting you go."

"Again with the caveman talk."

"I can beat my chest if you'd like."

She chuckles her perfect melody of laughter. "No, I've got the message."

I keep my hand on Devan's thigh the entire drive to the Dunns' farm. It's as if I have the basic, primitive, and innate need to be touching her. The sky overhead is a blanket of stars. With the truck's windows down, the summer night sounds create our soundtrack. Driving slowly down the lane toward Devan's house, crickets and toads sing their songs.

When I pull the truck up toward the garages, I cut the lights. "I'll take the blame if anyone questions why you came home so late."

Devan shakes her head. "I'm an adult, remember?"

My cheeks rise. "Yeah, that's not something I'm about to forget." I squeeze her thigh. "Stay there."

Opening my door, I hurry to the other side. Devan is a vision under the glow of the dome light. I open her door and offer her my hand. She steps down, her sandals landing on the gravel. As I lean down, ready to kiss her goodnight, I remember a text I received earlier today— well, now it was yesterday.

"I almost forgot."

"What?" she asks.

"Kandace texted me" —I shrug— "yesterday. She wondered if I could bring you to her and Dax's house Sunday afternoon."

Her lips curl. "I'd like that."

"Then it's a date."

Devan nods.

"I don't think I can wait until Sunday to see you again."

Her giggle is a tune I'll never tire of hearing.

"It's already Saturday," she says.

Taking her hand in mine, we walk the pathway to her porch. Gently cupping her cheek, I lean in for one last kiss. Our lips linger, both of us unwilling to say good night until fate and the clock refuse to let the night go further.

With a small step back, I say, "I had a great time."

"Me too."

I tilt my head. "Text me when you wake up. I'd like to see you."

She looks down at the bare flower beds. "I promised Mom I'd help her plant her annuals tomorrow." Her smile returns. "I'll text." She climbs the steps.

I wait until the door is open before I say, "Good night."

"Good night, Justin."

Chapter Twenty-Eight

Devan

Snapping the plastic lid in place, I secure the two quarts of fresh strawberries. They're cleaned, hulled, and delicious. Since I picked them this morning, I'm not sure they could be any fresher.

Ricky comes in the back door. Instead of heading up the stairs as he usually does, he pulls out a kitchen chair and sits.

"Hi," I say.

"I want to see your classroom."

"You do? Why?"

He smirks. "Justin told me about it, and I've been thinking. I'm a shit brother for not asking about your new job sooner."

"You're not a shit brother. You're busy. And I know

you and Dad are worried about what to do with the farm."

Ricky nods. "Yeah, there's a lot of shit happening." He leans back and his eyes scan me up and down. "Are you going somewhere?"

"Kandace Richards invited us to her house for lunch."

"Meeting the family."

"I've met the family, just not formally." I shrug. "Kandace came up to me at the softball game Thursday night."

"Have fun with that." He pushes his chair back, but before he stands, he sighs. "Do you like him?"

"I do."

My brother's lips are in a straight line as he nods. "I'm trying to come to terms with it..."

I'm about to comment that he has no say in the matter, but before I do, Ricky goes on.

"...And I think what I'm trying to say is there aren't many better guys out there than Justin."

I smile as a lump forms in my throat.

"That said, if he makes some dick move or does anything to upset you, I've got your back."

"Thank you." I remember something. "So you and Marilyn really kissed?"

"Shit." He shakes his head as he stands. "No."

Pursing my lips, I tilt my head.

"Okay, once."

"She's a great person too."

"She's going to grad school in the fall?" he asks.

I nod. "Finance."

His eyebrows raise. "Really? I didn't know she was into numbers."

I roll my eyes. "She's a genius with boring stuff."

Ricky stands. Switching the subject away from my friend to us, he asks, "Are we good?"

"Yeah. School doesn't start for three more weeks. Let me know when you can come by, and I'll show you the classroom."

"I will."

We both turn toward the window, hearing and seeing Justin's truck.

"Looks like your ride is here," Ricky says.

"He can still be your friend."

"He is. Don't make me choose because I don't want to."

"I don't plan on it," I say. When I look down at my top and shorts, I start to second-guess what I'm wearing.

As if he can read my mind, Ricky grins. "You look great. Have a good time."

I reach for the strawberries and my bag. "Thank you."

The back door opens.

"Hey," Justin says.

"Hi." I step closer and kiss his cheek. "I'll be right back." Handing Justin the strawberries, I hurry upstairs. The truth is that I don't have anything to do up here. I only want to give Justin and Ricky a minute to themselves. They both say everything is fine between them, but I worry.

Mom comes out of her room as I approach. "I thought you'd be gone."

I speak softly. "Justin is downstairs. Ricky was there." I shrug. "I wanted to give them a minute."

Mom's smile grows. "Honey, the boys will work out this new paradigm. You and Justin need to work out your relationship too. You aren't responsible for theirs." She reaches for my hand. "Thank you for all your help yesterday. The flowerbeds look fantastic."

"They do." I turn my hands until I can see my palms. "Even with gloves, I have blisters."

"Imagine what their hands are like," she says, tilting her head toward the back staircase.

Strong.

Rough.

Calloused.

Gentle.

As warmth fills my cheeks, I open my eyes wider, a bit nervous my expression is giving away my thoughts of what Justin's hands can do. "I guess it just goes to prove I'll leave the farming to them."

"Tell the Sheerses we send our love."

I lean my head. "We're going to the Richardses' house."

"I spoke with Bridget Sheers yesterday at the supermarket. Everyone will be at Kandace's. They're very happy about you and Justin."

My stomach drops. "Everyone?"

"Well, Justin's parents. You know, Bridget and Randy, and the Richardses, Dax, Kandace, and Molly."

"I didn't know about his parents."

"I guess now you're prepared. Just be you, honey. They'll love you. They already do."

"Why?"

"Because you make their son happy."

I bite my lower lip. "I want to."

"You do."

A quick look toward the back stairs. "I should go back down there." I brush her cheek with a kiss. "Bye, Mom."

"Have fun."

As I near the stairs, the sound of Justin's and Ricky's laughs eases a bit of my tension. It's good to hear them enjoying one another. They both turn as I appear from the stairs.

"What's so funny?" I ask.

Ricky looks at me. "Don't worry. I would never tell embarrassing stories about you."

"What?" My eyes open wide. "What stories?"

Justin reaches for my hand. "Come on, Kandace is waiting."

"What stories?" I ask again as we walk to his truck.

Justin laughs.

Once we're in the truck, I turn toward him. "Okay. Fair is fair. I'm going to ask Kandace for stories about you."

Justin shrugs as he backs up his truck. "You're going to find I am pretty boring. No big secrets in my closet."

"My closet doesn't have secrets. I don't know what Ricky told you, but I'm going to say he made it up."

Justin's lopsided grin grows. "You're saying you never had a panic attack on Pike's Peak?"

Jeez.

I shake my head. "I did. That's not embarrassing. It's science. Less oxygen to the brain because of the altitude."

"Science, okay."

"It is," I protest. "And I would have been fine if Dad and Ricky didn't want to go to the edge." I inhale. "Oh my God, thinking about it makes me queasy."

"Don't throw up in the truck," Justin says with a snicker. "I heard about the trashcan outside the shop at the top of the mountain."

"At least I made it to the trashcan. Some people didn't."

Justin reaches across the console to my leg. "Hey, it's all good fun."

I hum. "We'll see what I can learn from your sister." That reminds me. "Mom said she talked with your mom yesterday at the store, and she and your dad will be at Kandace's too."

His blue gaze comes my way and back to the road. "I didn't know that." He squeezes my knee. "Are you all right with that?"

"You've faced my family. Besides, Kandace spoke to

me at the softball game." I sit taller. "I'm excited to formally meet Molly."

"She's the best one of the family."

Kandace and Dax live in a grand old home at the edge of Riverbend city limits. In lieu of bricks, the exterior is covered with stone. It's one of those houses with a two-story middle and one-story wings to each side. The trim and two stately pillars on the front porch are yellow. When I was young, I always wondered what it looked like inside. I remember thinking it was a castle. Back then, it belonged to Dax's grandparents, the original owners of Quintessential Treasures.

I'm older. The house is less like a castle, but I'm still anxious to see inside.

Chapter Twenty-Nine

Devan

As Justin pulls his truck into their driveway and around to the back of the house where the garages and a basketball goal are, I ask, "Does your sister like living in town after living out on the farm her whole life?"

"You can ask her."

After opening my door, Justin takes my hand and leads me toward the back door near the garage.

"Should we go up front and ring the bell?"

Justin shakes his head. "Family doesn't ring the bell."

I think about that, about my parents' house. The front door is rarely even used. Everyone comes and goes through the kitchen.

At Kandace and Dax's house, the first door Justin takes me through leads into the garage. It's big enough for three cars, but the first stall is filled with a lawn mower, tools, and an array of bikes and riding toys. Through the next door, we enter a breezeway with windows and a door to the side yard. Up a few steps is another door. As we approach, I hear the voices inside.

"Are you sure you're ready?" Justin asks.

A smile comes to my lips. "If I said no, could we play hooky?"

"Without question. The Tastee Freeze is down the street."

"Hmm." I pretend to consider his offer. "I say we don't stand up your family, but" —I add— "I may take you up on the ice cream later."

"Deal." He leans close and kisses me. "That's for luck."

"Oh no. Do we need luck?"

As soon as Justin opens the door, Kandace and Mrs. Sheers's conversation stops, and both sets of eyes are on us. "Hello."

"Welcome."

Mrs. Sheers comes forward and wraps me in a hug. "Devan. It's so nice to see you."

"We're really glad you could make it," Kandace says.

"Thank you for inviting us," I say, stealing a peek at Justin who is grinning my direction. I extend my hand with the strawberries. "I picked these this morning."

Mrs. Sheers takes the bowl. "Oh, there's nothing better than fresh-picked strawberries. Thank you."

"You're welcome, Mrs. Sheers."

"Oh no. That was my mother-in-law, God rest her soul. I'm Bridget, and Justin's father is Randy."

"I'm Molly."

We all turn toward a swinging door at the end of the kitchen, still moving from Molly's entrance. I would know Molly Richards anyway. She has the same shade of hair as her mom and uncle and her dad's golden eyes.

"Who are you?" she asks, straight to the point.

"Molly," Justin says, crouching down. "Come here."

The little girl squeals as she runs into his arms, and he lifts her off the ground. Still holding her, he says, "This is my friend Devan."

"You have friends?"

Everyone laughs.

With a chuckle in my voice, I reply, "He does. I'm his friend. May I be your friend too?"

Molly glances toward her mother for permission. From the corner of my eye, I see Kandace nod. Molly sticks out her hand. "Hi, Devan, I'm Molly, and we can be friends."

Shaking her little hand, I grin. "It's official."

Justin sets her feet back on the ground and she reaches for his hand. "Uncle Justin, come see what Dad made."

"Dax made something?" he says to Kandace.

"It is a time of miracles." Her gaze goes to me. "Devan, please make yourself at home. You can stay with Mom and me or go with Justin. Whatever you'd like."

"I'm curious about Mr. Richards's creation."

"Dax," Kandace says.

"What Dax made."

Following a step behind Justin and Molly, I pass through the swinging door to the dining room. Off to the right is a large living room with windows looking out on a stunningly green lawn with a large swing set. Taking another right, we pass through glass doors to a sunroom. It's outside the sunroom that I see where Molly is taking Justin.

Dax and Mr. Sheers—Randy—are already outside. Built into the tree overhead is a small house. A tree house.

"Is that for you?" Justin asks Molly.

She nods her head quickly. "It has a rope ladder, but" —her little nose scrunches— "I'm not good at that yet. So, Dad put up the real ladder."

"Can I see inside?" Justin asks after a casual greeting to Dax and Randy.

"Do you want to?"

"I do."

Molly turns to me. "Devan, do you want to see inside my tree house, too?"

"Very much."

"Dad," Molly asks, "can I take them up there?"

Dax's voice is deep like Justin's. "I think that will fill it to capacity, but you should make it."

"Capacity?" Molly asks.

Justin crouches to her level. "It means we might fill it up, but we'll all fit." When Justin stands, he wraps his arm around my lower back. "Dad, Dax, this is Devan." He looks at me. "My dad and brother-in-law."

"Welcome, Devan."

"Nice to meet you. I'm Randy by the way."

"Nice to meet you," I say.

Dax moves the ladder and watches closely as Molly makes her way to the top. The tree house is probably at least eight feet off the ground. I can't imagine using a rope ladder. Justin motions for me to go next. I do, bending at the top to fit through the doorway. Justin is not far behind me.

"How do you like it?" Molly asks.

The inside walls are painted bright yellow, the ceiling white, and the flooring is actual flooring, the vinyl that's meant to look like wood. There is a beanbag chair and a small table with two chairs. The windows even have flowy white curtains.

"Molly," I say, "this is beautiful."

She sticks her hand out one of the windows. "There isn't glass, but if I pull this string a door closes. It keeps the rain and snow out."

Justin sticks his head out the doorway. "Nice job, Richards. Your carpentry skills are improving."

From where I am, I can see Dax's middle finger. It makes both Justin and me laugh.

After a more detailed tour, we all take turns climbing down the ladder. Whatever nerves I might have had about today's gathering are totally gone by the time we all sit down to eat. Instead of eating at the big dining room table, Kandace and Bridget bring the food to the sunroom. Currently, the glass doors are open and it's like a big screen porch.

"Tell us, Devan," Kandace begins, "how you convinced this confirmed bachelor that there is more to life than farming and being awful at softball."

"I'm not awful," Justin says.

"He did hit the only home run last week," I add.

Kandace rolls her eyes.

Before I can answer, Justin does. "She kissed me."

I choke on my iced tea as Bridget's eyes widen.

"There's a little more to it," I say.

"We're all ears," Kandace says.

Swallowing my tea, I say, "He didn't know who I was. It was at the Gordons' hog roast."

Dax leans back. "That was you?"

Justin nods.

"Man, he was talking about you for weeks. No one else saw you."

I reply, "I didn't tell anyone I was in town."

Justin chimes in. "I later learned she was here for her interview with Cory."

"Even Cory didn't know who you were talking about," Dax says.

Justin turns my way with a sexy grin. "I couldn't believe no one else saw her. I couldn't forget her."

"Okay," Kandace says. "Now get to the good part. When did he figure out who you were? Or are, I should say."

I go on to tell them the story of Marilyn's dad being called into work. Justin taking his place. How he pretended not to recognize me. Even Randy is laughing when I tell them about the open windows and slamming doors. I leave out the part about the fortuitous moving tote.

"I guess," Justin says, "you can say the rest is history."

"That reminds me," I say. "Since Justin and Ricky have known one another their whole lives, I'm going to need some dirt to hold over his head, things he did as a child."

Kandace laughs. "Oh, I have hours of material. We may need wine." She pouts. "No wine for me."

There is that rumor.

"Congratulations," I say.

Her smile beams. "Thank you. We weren't exactly trying."

"We weren't not trying," Dax adds.

It's Randy Sheers who holds up his hands. "Not a conversation for a dad to hear." He clutches his chest with a grin. "Remember, your old man has a bad heart."

"Your heart is the best," Bridget says. She stands. "Devan brought fresh strawberries, and I found vanilla ice cream in the freezer. Who wants some?"

Everyone says yes.

I stand up to help with clearing the table when Justin reaches for my arm. "You don't have to help."

"You help at my house. I want to."

It feels right to help Kandace and Bridget. They're

fun and keep the conversation light. After the ice cream and strawberries, I worry I will need to undo the button on my shorts. Justin and I stay a while, talking, watching Molly, and having a nice afternoon.

As we're driving toward my house, Justin asks, "How do you feel about a weekend getaway?"

Chapter Thirty

Justin

"Is it too soon?" I ask. "I know we haven't been official long, but I feel like this all started a few months ago, at the hog roast. I was thinking, since neither one of us has our own place, maybe we could spend some time..." I peer to my side.

Devan is smiling.

Lowering my chin to my chest, I mumble, "Word-vomit."

Her giggle rings through the cab of my truck. "I'm beginning to catch on. You talk fast and say a lot when you're nervous."

Straightening my neck, I clench my jaw. "I'm not nervous."

Devan reaches over and lays her fingers on my arm. "No. Big, grumpy Justin Sheers is never nervous."

A laugh ruins my attempt at a gruff exterior. I turn my focus away from the road to see her beautiful face. "I'm not nervous with you. I just don't want to fuck this up. Like today."

"What about today?"

"You fit in with my family like you are meant to be there. I feel the same way about yours." I take a deep breath. "For the record, this isn't about to be more word-vomit."

"Okay," she says with a giggle.

"It's that I never even imagined dating, serious dating, exclusive dating. It was totally off my radar. And then we kissed. Shit, I've known you for most of your life, but I didn't really. Don't really. I want to. I didn't truly see you until that night by the pond. I think it's why no one, including Ricky, recognized the woman I described." I swallow and reach my hand over to her leg. "Devan, I see you in a way that is so damn special. Maybe I was blind before or just not paying attention. Now, each time I see you, talk to you, touch you" —I squeeze her leg— "I'm blown away that you want to date me."

"I feel the same way."

"Are you kidding? You're gorgeous, fun, a damn hard worker, and sexy beyond belief. I'm thinking about packing a handgun, just in case any other man thinks he has a chance with you."

"I don't think that's necessary." She lays her hand over mine. "I'm not looking at another man. Away?" she asks. "To where and when?"

"Would you believe me that I haven't thought that far ahead. I wasn't sure you'd say yes."

"Yes, Justin. I know what you mean about being soon and yet not feeling like we're rushing it. I get it. After the other night, after you took me home, I thought about how nice it would be to still be in your arms, to sleep beside you, and to wake with you."

"We're on the same page," I say. "Can we rule out that hotel in Bloomington?"

"Yes."

We both laugh.

"How far away?" I ask. "Should I look into plane tickets?"

"That's unnecessary. Besides, are we going to go sightseeing or do you have other plans?"

"I haven't worked out all the details, but I'm thinking other plans."

"My answer is yes," she says. "You can surprise me."

My mind is filled with possibilities.

Something special.

Something romantic.

Something out of my comfort zone.

Instead of taking Devan straight home, we head to a spot I know by a lake. It's only a few miles out of town. There's no public beach, but some friends of my folks have a house there and have given our family an open invitation.

"Where are we going?"

"Boggs Lake."

"Are you kidnapping me?"

A smile lifts my cheeks. "I think I am. I'm not ready to take you home." I turn my hand palm up, the one on her leg. Devan places her hand in mine.

I park behind the Howards' garage. After a few knocks, we determine they aren't home.

"Are you sure this is okay?" Devan asks.

"My parents have been friends with the Howards forever. Besides, we're only going to go down to their dock."

Taking Devan's hand, I walk her along the side of the house. This isn't where the Howards live year around, but they're usually here in the summer. From what I can see through the windows, everything looks the same. They could be out for a Sunday drive. We walk through their carport, pass a sprawling elevated deck, and walk down a narrow staircase that leads through a patch of trees to the waterfront.

Green grass covers the lawn up to a seawall. People can either walk out on the dock or take the steps down to the sandy shore.

At the edge of the lawn, Devan stops and lifts her chin. The breeze off the lake blows wisps of her yellow hair around her beautiful face. Unable to resist, I lean over and brush her lips with mine.

The sunlight sparkles in her eyes as she hums. "This is beautiful."

We take off our shoes and sit on the edge of the dock, letting our feet soak in the fresh, cool water. I tell her how I learned to water-ski on this lake. I'm also confident that my many attempts to get up on top of the water on skis is part of Kandace's embarrassing stories.

Devan shares how she learned to water-ski and her love of Jet Skis. As we sit, we talk about things I haven't thought of in years. It amazes me how easy it is to talk with her. Most people would probably say I'm quiet. Around Devan it's the exact opposite. That doesn't mean that I don't give her a chance to share. I do, listening to every word she says.

It's after seven when we put back on our shoes and trek up the hill and stairs.

"Justin," Mr. Howard calls from the deck as we get closer. While I think of the Howards as my parents' friends, they are older than my parents. Mr. Howard's hair is snow-white, and his frame has lessened with time.

"Mr. Howard," I reply. Once we're to the deck level, I introduce Devan.

"Nice to meet you, young lady."

Devan's cheeks are pink from our day in the sun. "Nice to meet you."

"Would you like some lemonade," he asks.

"I need to get Devan home," I reply.

"Maybe next time. You two come back and take the boat out. I'm getting too old for those stairs, and it could use a good running."

Holding Devan's hand, I say, "Thank you. That sounds like a great offer."

"What is your week like?" I ask Devan once we're back in the truck and headed for the Dunn farm.

"Lesson plans."

"Sounds fun."

"Your week?" she asks.

I flash her a smile. "Planning your surprise weekend getaway."

"That sounds like fun."

After dropping Devan off and kissing her goodbye, I call my brother-in-law. I usually call Ricky for advice. However, asking him where a good place would be to take his sister's virginity doesn't seem like a good call. It sounds like a call that could end with me in the depths of one of the quarries.

"Sheers," Dax answers. "What's happening?"

"You met Devan."

"Yeah, she was here a few hours ago. Is your memory going?"

"Shut up," I say. "It was a segue."

"Oh." He laughs.

"Forget it. I'll call someone else."

"No. No. What can I do for you? Is this about the Dunn farm?"

"No." I'd rather not think about that right now. "I need some advice." Before he could make another asinine comment, I go on, "I want to take Devan away for the weekend. I want someplace special."

"You're asking me because Kandace has told you what a great romantic I am, right?"

"No, asshole. I'm asking you because Kandace seems to be putting up with you and your shit, so you must be doing something right."

Dax laughs. "A few months ago, when we found out Kandace was pregnant, we went down to West Baden. It was a great weekend. Although, they book up fast, especially this time of year."

West Baden Spring Hotel.

I hadn't thought of it.

The hotel is famous and historic. Some even say it's haunted.

"I'll give them a shot," I say. "Thank you."

"Hey," Dax says. "This caring about someone looks good on you. Don't blow it."

It's my turn to laugh. "I'm trying not to. Thanks for the vote of confidence."

As soon as I hang up and I pull into our farm near our garages, I look up West Baden Springs Hotel and click the website.

<h1 style="text-align:center">Chapter Thirty-One</h1>

Devan

Justin and I talk throughout the week, but we don't see one another until Thursday's softball game. I spend my week slammed with creating lesson plans and integrating the changes the science department has adopted. Instead of working at the school, I've taken full advantage of Mom's old craft room—my new office. I have a beautiful view of the fields and a great breeze if I move out to the back patio.

Being a visual person, I outline the assignment, complete it, create and practice an associated hands-on experiment, and then type my notes in detail. I'm sure not everyone is putting this effort into their lesson plans, but it isn't their first year of teaching either.

Justin has been busy too. While his fields are all planted, there is constant work with irrigation, fertilization, and fumigation. He told me a horror story about an infestation of seed-corn maggots not long after he graduated Purdue. From a science perspective, I'm fascinated with the fortitude of the seed-corn maggot. There are no treatments to rescue a corn crop after infestation. Their eggs hatch in two to four days with four to five generations per year. Their rapid regeneration would be a model if they weren't so destructive. From a farming perspective, I remember when the last infestation happened. Since there's no treatment, infected corn must be tilled over and replanted. The adding of beneficial nematodes has shown to be helpful, but this must be done at the time of planting.

I'm impressed with how much Justin knows about the land.

He says he's not willing to lose another crop to the seed-corn maggots. Knowing that increased moisture can trigger the perfect environment for the devastating insects, and that our area had increased precipitation this past spring, Justin and his dad added the nematodes before planting.

The nematodes are basically worms that help to regulate the populations of other soil organisms. Some of the farms who didn't add the beneficial worms are seeing the maggots.

Tilling entire fields, adding nematodes, and replanting is not only expensive, it delays the crop's development, moving harvest to later in the year. That creates a whole new list of issues. The good news is that the

Sheerses' corn is healthy. Justin said Dad and Ricky's crop is too. Justin may have taken credit for convincing Ricky to add the nematodes. It's not something I plan to ask my brother.

At Thursday's game, Justin makes the same climb, kissing me before the first pitch. It seems like there are fewer eyes upon us. Unfortunately, for Thursday's game, the good-luck kisses don't pay off. Trevor, a nearby town, wins by a score of seven to four.

Now it is Friday, and I'm excited for our weekend away.

All I know about where we're going is to pack a few dresses for dinner, a bathing suit for the spa and pool, and...

Justin says no other clothing is required.

For the record, I pack more than he requested. I pack a nightgown that I picked up in a boutique in Indianapolis when Jill and I went to drop off some of her things off at Todd's apartment one afternoon. I also pack underwear because of Justin's fair warning about consequences in announcing I'm not wearing any.

After Justin informed me that we had reservations for a weekend away, I did the adult thing and told my mom the truth. To my surprise, she took it better than I anticipated. She said I've lived on my own—with Marilyn —for four years. She accepts that I'm not a child and to please let her know when we arrive safely.

It's almost five thirty in the afternoon when through the living room windows, I see the dust cloud on our lane coming from Justin's truck. To be honest, I've thought so much about this weekend, I'm about ready to jump out of my own skin.

My packed bags are waiting by the door, and I'm dressed in the same sundress I wore the night we went to the quarry.

"Where are you going?" Ricky asks when he enters the house and sees my bags.

Yeah, I didn't tell him.

"I don't know," I say with a smile.

"You don't know?"

Ricky turns to see Justin's truck coming to a stop near the garages. "Wait. You're going away with Justin?"

"Yes."

"Does Mom know?"

"She does."

"Dad?"

"I'd assume so."

Ricky runs his hand over his hair. "How long will you be gone? Why do you have a suitcase?"

Walking to the door, I grab the handle of my suitcase, put my floppy hat on my head and grin. "I'll see you Sunday."

Pushing open the door, I see Justin's panty-melting smile as he walks toward me. After nearly a week of being apart with only seeing him briefly at the game, all six-feet-plus of him looking at me the way he is currently is a sight for sore eyes. As stunningly handsome as ever,

Justin's stare intensifies, warming my skin more than the summer heat.

"Hi," he says with a kiss.

Dropping the suitcase, I lift my arms to his shoulders, savoring the sensation of my body against his. This kiss is longer and deeper, twisting my core. My heart pounds against his chest. "Hi."

"Are you ready for our adventure?"

"Are you going to tell me where we're going?" I ask.

The screen door slams.

We both turn toward the house.

Ricky's forehead is furrowed, and his hands are buried deep in his pockets.

"Hey," Justin says.

"I saw you at breakfast." Removing his hand, Ricky gestures about. "You never mentioned this."

Justin smiles. "Was I supposed to ask Devan out or you?"

Ricky walks down the steps until he's close. "Remember how pissed you were when you found out Kandace was pregnant?"

"Whoa," I say, lifting my hand.

Ricky isn't looking at me. He's focused on Justin. "Don't do that."

Instead of getting upset, Justin looks at me and grins. "I guess it's plan B." He picks up my suitcase with one hand and takes my hand in his other.

"What is plan B?" Ricky calls after us.

I'm laughing as Justin helps me into his truck. Before

shutting the door, he leans in and gives me a kiss. "You're beautiful, and I've missed seeing and touching you all week."

"You're handsome, and I've missed you, too." My eyebrows quirk. "What is plan B?"

"It's taken me all week to work out plan A. I'm not turning back now."

There's something in his blue orbs that makes my stomach do flip-flops.

Once Justin is seated behind the steering wheel, I ask, "How long to our destination?"

"Less than an hour."

"You decided on the Bloomington hotel?"

"No." He laughs. "We're headed southeast."

I picture the state. "Are we going to Lexington?" That is out of state, but it's southeast.

"Nope," he says, backing his truck up and turning around.

Evansville is southwest.

Indianapolis is northeast.

St. Louis is west.

Before pulling out of our lane, Justin puts his truck in park. "Come closer."

"I'm kind of stuck in my seat belt."

He tilts his head. "Get unstuck. Come closer, and I'll give you a hint."

"My curiosity is piqued." I unfasten my seat belt and lean over the console. "What is my hint?"

Cupping my cheek, Justin kisses me—full-out,

panty-melting kiss, complete with tongue. Unlike either kiss at my house, this one continues, warming me from the inside and sparking nerves that only he has been able to ignite. A butterfly kiss and a lick of my lips.

"Did you just lick me?"

When Justin pulls back, he has a devilish grin. "Where are we going?" he asks.

"That was my hint?" My mind is too scrambled to make sense. "It was a kiss. It was a great kiss..."

He tilts his head toward my seat belt. "Buckle up, buttercup."

I'm trying to put the clues together as I fasten my seat belt. And then it hits me.

Kiss with tongue.

French kiss.

A lick.

"We're going to French Lick," I squeal. "Oh my God, West Baden?"

Justin nods.

"I've never been there."

He reaches over and takes my hand. "It will be a first for both of us."

Chapter Thirty-Two

Devan

On our drive, I look up the history of the West Baden Hotel. And read aloud.

It was built in 1845 and patterned after fancy European spas. In 1888, it was bought by Lee W. Sinclair who transformed it into a sophisticated resort with many amenities including a ball field and double-decker track—for ponies and bicycles. In 1901, the building was ravaged by fire. Sinclair used the opportunity to make it even better with the world's largest free-span dome.

After the stock-market crash of 1929, the hotel was sold for one dollar. It became a seminary for thirty years, removing all the elegant features. A college then used the hotel from 1967 to 1983. And then afterward, the magnificent structure sat empty for thirteen years. In

1991, a 180-foot, six-story section collapsed. The hotel received the attention of a nonprofit preservation group. The refurbished hotel and casino opened in November of 2006.

"I had no idea it had all that history," Justin said.

"Do you think that's why some people think it's haunted?"

Justin laughed. "I reserved a room for two. If the room is haunted, the ghosts will need to find somewhere else to stay."

I continued reading. "It looks like people think the first owner, a guy named Taggart, is still hanging around, despite dying in 1916."

"If you're scared, I promise to keep you safe."

"My hero."

The historic hotel is bigger than I imagined, looking like a castle as we approach. Together we walk into the gigantic lobby. The room is round with tall pillars and a beautiful high ceiling, the combination of which making me feel small. Even Justin's height is dwarfed by the size of the room. I stand to his side as he checks us in. His words don't register as I look around with the weight of what accepting this weekend getaway invitation truly means.

I peer up at his profile.

Justin Sheers.

At times like these, it almost seems as if I'm in a dream. It's hard to fathom that this man, one I've known most of my life, is the man I want to share my life with.

Yes, I'm thinking about more than my body. I want that too. I want to enjoy the way he makes me feel. I also don't want to stop with giving him my virginity.

In the short time since our one kiss, I realize I want to share my life with him. I never dreamed we would have such similar interests—mine of earth science and his of geology and farming, or that it would be so easy to talk to him, or that his smile would make the dark clouds part and fill my life with sunshine.

As Ricky's little sister, I never took the time to witness the sweet, sincere, and sexual side of Justin Sheers. Maybe he never showed it. Knowing he's sharing it with me now adds to the way he makes me feel special.

Now that I've not only seen the hidden sides but witnessed them firsthand in his kiss, touch, and kindness, I believe I could spend the next fifty years learning every side, level, and layer to this handsome man.

"Devan?"

I shake my head with a giggle. "Sorry, I think I was spacing out."

"Did you see a ghost?"

"No." I'm not thinking about an apparition from the past but about what possibilities the future holds.

We both pull our suitcases across the shiny marble floor as Justin takes my hand. Once in the elevator, Justin hits the button for the fourth floor. The furnishings throughout the hotel are lavish, reminding me of something out of a movie. When he opens the door to our suite, I laugh. Yeah, maybe it's nerves.

"Is this funny?" he asks.

Letting go of my suitcase, I spin around, my arms outstretched. "It's not funny. And it's so not that hotel in Bloomington." The room may be the nicest one I've ever stayed in.

Justin's smile shines. "Come look." He tugs my hand. "We have an atrium view."

Beyond our windows, there is a large dome covering a spectacular room below with clusters of seats and guests milling from here to there.

Turning back to Justin, I grin. "This is beautiful."

"You, Devan, are beautiful. This is a nice hotel."

"It's still beautiful," I insist.

"Before your stomach starts growling," Justin says with a smirk, "where would you like to eat? I have reservations for tomorrow night at Sinclair's Restaurant."

"He was the guy in the history."

"That's probably where they got the name," he says. "I thought maybe tonight we could walk around. Check things out. Find someplace to dine."

"I thought you said we weren't sightseeing."

He cups my cheek.

It's a habit I'm growing to love, to lean into his warm, firm touch.

"Sightsee tonight," he says, "while you're still wearing clothes. Remember, other than dinner tomorrow or maybe going out to the pool, we are on a clothes-free getaway."

"You plan to starve me?" I ask with added dramatic flair.

"Room service."

My smile grows. "You thought of everything." I don't want to wait. I've waited twenty-two years and never has it felt this right. The sights will be there tomorrow. Taking a step back, I veil my eyes and push one of the spaghetti straps off my shoulder.

"Devan." His timbre is lower than moments before.

I push the strap off the other shoulder.

"Do you know what you're doing?"

"Plan B," I say with a smile.

Justin comes closer and lifts my chin. Within his blue orbs, I see the brewing of a storm. It's mesmerizing and intense. The summer thunderstorm that grows in the humid air, no warning, and no way to know what it has in store.

His voice is deep and soft. "I want you to know there is no pressure."

"There is. I feel it. Not from you but when I'm with you. From that one kiss, when we're together, my entire body feels as if it could implode at any moment. I've never felt this way before. I thought the feeling would dwindle, but it hasn't, Justin. It's more intense every time we talk, you reach for my hand, or we kiss."

He sighs. "I'm fucking petrified I'm going to scare you away, but damn it, I like you—I think I love you. I'm not saying that to get into your pants."

Love.

I concentrate on the last part of his statement. "You've already been there."

"Yeah," he says with a smirk. "I want to go back, but that isn't why I'm saying this. I don't know how you see us. I see us lasting for a long time. That means we can spend this weekend doing what we've done, holding one another, talking, and I might even allow clothes and sightseeing. We don't need to go all the way. I'm not going anywhere. If we do it this weekend or a week from now or a year, Devan, I'm in this for the long haul."

"I want to do all those things you said. I didn't save my virginity for some extravagant occasion. I just have never wanted to go that far with anyone. Riverbend… before, there was no one I wanted to have that experience with. No one I thought of as my forever. Until now."

Justin's eyes close as he exhales. When he opens them, the storm clouds from earlier are replaced with the igniting of flames, ice-blue embers that are combusting into a raging fire. His voice takes on a gravelly tenor. "What do you want?"

"You, Justin. I want you. I think I love you too. Maybe it's lust, but it feels like more than that—more than I've felt. It feels exciting, new, and at the same time, comfortable. Does that make sense?"

He nods. His gaze lingers on my lowered straps. "I can either help you push those back up or take that dress all the way off. If we go with the latter, I think room service is in our future."

"How about we build up an appetite first?"

I don't need to ask twice before we are on each other. It isn't as if I have no idea how to proceed. As Justin lifts my dress over my head, I lift his shirt over his. This isn't going to be a fast wham-bam-thank-you-ma'am. I want to even the playing field.

That means that Justin too will be without clothes.

No boxer shorts.

Nothing.

As our different items of clothing make it to the carpet, our hands skirt over one another's flesh. Justin's touch is everywhere: my arms, sides, breasts, and behind. I hold onto what he told me before—to be bold.

Running my fingertips over his broad shoulders, thick arms, and toned torso, I savor every indentation, every muscle, every inch of his massive body. As his boxer shorts are kicked away, I have a moment of trepidation. In principle, I understand the mechanics of sex. That said, I worry he's too big or maybe I'm not big enough.

Justin reaches for my shoulders. "No rush."

Nodding, I fall to my knees and look up at him through my veiled lashes.

"Fuck, Devan. You don't have to do that."

Seizing his cock between both of my hands, I marvel at the girth and length. Running my touch up the shaft, I'm surprised by the velvety yet hard surface. Small veins pop to life as he grows harder and thicker under my touch. Pre-come shimmers on the tip. Without thinking, I lean in and lick the tip.

My taste buds sense the saltiness.

Justin's growl stops me.

"Am I doing this wrong?"

His jaw is clenched and his Adam's apple bobs. "Fuck no. Your tongue is perfect. I'm sure your mouth is too." He reaches for my chin and encourages me to stand. "Other than our dry humping and some cold showers, it's been a while for me too. Before I come in your sexy mouth, I want to come in your pussy...if you're ready."

"Condoms?"

Justin nods.

As he did in Bloomington, he flips back the top cover from the king-sized bed. Next, he finds his blue jeans from the floor, takes his wallet from his pocket, and fishes out a condom.

"Did you bring more than one?"

He grins. "In the suitcase."

Nodding, I scoot up on the bed, reach out my hand, and ask, "Can I do it?"

His sexy blue eyes roll. "You're killing me."

"I promise that's not my goal."

He hands me the packet. While I've never seen one in real life, it's not rocket science. I rip open the packet with my teeth—my dental hygienist mother would be more upset about that than the sex—and I hold the condom in my grasp. It's round and looks like a rolled-up balloon.

My heart beats too fast as I place it on the end of his cock and roll the length over him. "Do they ever break?"

As he reaches for my shoulders, he says, "If it does, we can tell Ricky we tried."

Directing me, Justin lays me against the pillows.

I spread my knees and stare up at the ceiling, trying to ignore my racing pulse and sudden onset of nerves.

"Devan," he says, his tone soft and tenor low. "Look at me."

My gaze goes to him.

"You're overthinking this."

"I mean…it's a lot to think about." My focus goes to his cock. "A lot."

Justin grins and offers me his hand. "Come here."

"Where?"

"Here, Devan. Come to me."

On the giant mattress, we're both on our hands and knees. Justin starts with kisses. My lips, my ear, my neck. With each kiss, my tension eases and my skin warms. Despite the rise in temperature, my flesh blankets in goosebumps.

Encouraging me to sit up, he lowers his attention to my breasts. It's not simple sucking. Hell, I'm not even sure what he's doing, but whatever it is I feel it from my hardened nipples to my twisting core.

Moans and whimpers escape me as the luxurious hotel room disappears. I'm not sure when it happens, when I lie back on the bed, but as Justin's kisses move over my stomach and toward my core, I feel as if I'm an old-fashion top, spun tighter and tighter, about to lose control.

I cry out as his tongue laps my sensitive flesh and swirls my clit. One finger and then two, so long and the perfect amount of coarseness. My heart is aflutter as my body processes his rhythm. In and out. My back arches and my neck stretches as I push up with my heels.

For only a millisecond, his touch is gone, and then he's over me. His lips on mine, his tongue coated with my essence dances with mine. As he distracts me with his amazing kisses, I'm aware of the pressure, his hard cock at my entrance. My eyes open. The swirling blue in Justin's orbs is truly hypnotizing. As I stare, my body relaxes.

This is where I want to be.

I'm with who I want to be with.

I grimace and grasp his shoulders as he pushes through the barrier I saved for this man.

He wipes a tear from my cheek. "Are you all right?" he asks.

I nod.

"Look at me, Devan."

My eyes open wide.

"Thank you." His kisses flutter over my lips, face, and neck as he begins to move. Gently, he's thrusting in and out. The initial stretch has waned, the soreness is forgotten. The top within me is back to being wound, and I'm about to spin out of control.

Chapter Thirty-Three

Justin

Devan is absolutely stunning and so fucking tight. While I've had sex before, everything about this is different. Everything about being with Devan is unique. I can't ignore how great it feels to be inside her, but that isn't my main thought. I want her to enjoy it. I want to make it the best for her.

The worry in her gaze when she first lay on the bed is gone. Damn, the way she's looking at me is overwhelming. "Are you all right?" I ask again as I slow my thrusts.

"Better than all right," she says, her smile dazzling. "I didn't know I'd feel so full."

I start to back away. "Is it too much?"

Devan's arms wrap around my lower back. "Don't stop, Justin." Her neck elongates as she brings her lips to mine.

My goal is to take it easy and slow; however, with each thrust, each push deeper, each easing out, I'm on the brink of coming. Taking a breath, I still my movements. When Devan opens her eyes, I ask, "Do you ever touch yourself?"

The mortification on her expression, considering our intimate position, is cute.

"Do it."

"What?"

"Do it, touch yourself. Roll your clit."

"I-I..."

I kiss her lips. "Do it for me. I want to watch you come."

The indecision in her eyes fades as she moves one hand between us. I begin again, in and out. Perspiration coats our skin as our bodies slap together. Her hand moves faster. It's as her eyes roll back that I pick up speed.

"Oh, Justin," she calls out as her pussy convulses.

I've lasted as long as I could. Grasping her hips, I hold tight as my cock is strangled, draining my seed. Holding myself above her, I wait for her to focus, to see me. When she does, her milk-chocolate stare swirls with the ecstasy of satiation.

"I do love you, Devan."

"I love you, too."

As I start to pull out, her smile fades.

"Talk to me," I say. "You can always talk to me."

"Is this real, or on Monday will it be over now that we did this?"

Pulling out, I reach for her and roll us until she's over me. My still-erect dick is sandwiched between us, and she's lying between my legs. I frame her beautiful face with the palms of my hands. "If you think I'd do that, that I'd leave you because I got what I wanted, you don't know me."

She tips her forehead to my shoulder. "I don't want to think that way."

I lift her face. "Here's the thing, Devan. I like—okay, more than like—what I just got, but that doesn't mean I've gotten what I want from you."

"What do you want?"

"Only forever. And it will take a long time for me to get that. The only way this, between us, is ending is if you think I'm too clingy and you walk away."

Devan lays her head on my shoulder. "Forever?"

I nod.

When she lifts her head and our gazes meet, her stunning smile is back. "I don't mind clingy if it's someone I want to be with."

"Do you want to be with me?" I ask.

"Only forever."

I read about the amenities of the West Baden Hotel. Other than Saturday night's dinner at Sinclair's, the amenity we enjoyed the most was room service. Just because this was Devan's first time, it didn't stop her from it being her second, third, fourth...I lost count. We spent our getaway doing more than simple sex.

Lying naked, we fed one another grapes and French

fries—dipped in mayo. And it wasn't gross. We showered together, only for that to culminate in Devan's first experience at shower sex. The nights and days melded together as one of us would wake the other with kisses and caresses. When I packed, I never expected to run out of condoms.

I didn't, but it was close.

On Sunday morning, we looked around the room.

"I hear it's a nice hotel," I say.

Devan laughs. "I guess we could have gone back to Bloomington."

I shake my head, snaking my arm around her and pulling her to me. "Do you know how many people have lost their virginity in the Gordon hayloft?"

"Is there an actual registry somewhere?"

"No." I swat her round ass—something I learned she doesn't hate.

"Hey."

"You love my hand on your ass."

Pink fills her cheeks. "I do. Now back to your statement. Am I supposed to calculate throughout time or in the last decade? Do you know when the barn was built?"

Snagging her chin, I bring her lips to mine. "The question was rhetorical."

Her lips curl. "Oh, well, then no. I don't know."

"I didn't want that for you. You saved a wonderful part of yourself and chose to share it with me." I look around the room. "I wanted it to be special."

Devan leans into me. "It was but not because of the

room. It was special because of you."

"Good," I say. "Since we're headed back to River-bend where neither of us have our own place, we may end up in the hayloft."

Devan giggles.

That gets me thinking.

I'm thirty-two years old. It's time I get a place of my own.

Walking Devan to her door, to the Dunns' back door, I kiss her again. "Thank you for an amazing weekend."

She nods. "I think I need a nap."

"Call me tonight?"

Her cheeks rise. "You are clingy."

"Only in a good way."

Her nap sounds like a great idea until I drive up to my house and see Jack Dunn's truck parked outside.

Clenching my jaw, I walk into the house, listening for voices. They're coming from Dad's office. For a moment, I stand outside the closed door. The voices are muffled. Without a knock, I open the door and am met by Dad and Jack.

"What's happening?" I ask, assessing the mood.

It's not jovial.

"Come in, Justin," Dad says. He looks to Jack. "You can fill him in."

Jack sighs. "Janet has carpal tunnel."

"Is that bad?" I ask.

"It can be treated with surgery. Thing is, she is ready

to retire. I am too."

I nod. This isn't new news.

"The developer, he came by yesterday with his best offer yet. He'll pay us now and let us live on the property through the winter. We can even harvest. We just need to be out by the end of March."

"Where will you go? What about Devan and Ricky?"

"Janet and I have been talking. We can buy a house in town. We're wanting to go someplace warm, but the kids can live there, and we'll have a place to stay when we visit."

"Have you told them?" I ask, knowing I've been with Devan all weekend.

"Ricky knows," Jack says.

I pace back and forth, a million thoughts in my head. The biggest is that I don't want Devan to have a reason to leave Riverbend. If her family is gone, will she want to move away?

"Is it a set deal?" I ask.

Jack shakes his head. "I gave you my word, Justin, that I'd talk to you and Randy first. That's why I'm here."

My gaze moves to my dad. There are so many things I want to say. At the same time, with Jack and Janet getting their freedom, I can't ask my parents to mortgage the farm. They deserve to travel, to live outside of Riverbend.

"Jack," Dad says, "can Justin and I have a little while to talk? I promise you an answer by the end of the day."

Jack nods. "I'll be waiting."

Dad walks with Jack out to his truck as I go to the kitchen and drain a water bottle. When Dad comes back in, I say, "I can't ask you to go into debt for my dream."

"You didn't ask me. Your mom and I have talked about it. We hate that damn developer. We don't want all the traffic and water issues. The Dunn farm isn't huge, but if we can save it for another generation, we want to do it."

I take a deep breath. "I told Ricky I wanted to buy the farm before Devan and I kissed. I want you to know this didn't start out as something about her."

"Is it now?"

I nod. "It's way too fucking early, but I love her, Dad. If we can offer the Dunns the same deal, let them harvest and stay in the house until spring—it doesn't have to be March. Maybe next spring, Devan and I can live in their house."

"With Ricky?"

I laugh. "No, that's not the plan. He wants to go back to school. Once they're through harvest, he can start exploring his options."

"That's a lot of maybes."

My smile grows. "No maybes, Dad. I'll work my ass off to keep both farms—correction, the Sheers farm, bigger than before—working and profitable. As for Devan, I think that's more than a maybe too."

"You want to drive with me over to the Dunns' and make the offer?"

"I was just there. Might as well go back."

Chapter Thirty-Four

Justin

Six months later

"You know it's freezing outside?" Ricky asks for probably the fifth time.

"I don't care. It's where we went on our first date."

"You couldn't have taken her to a restaurant or someplace with heat."

"Shut up," I say, sending a scowl toward my best friend. "I want this to be special. And I think Devan will want her friends to be there as part of it—make it official. I know I do."

Ricky shakes his head. "Devan is turning you soft."

The truth is the exact opposite, but I'm not going to point that out to her brother.

"Just be there. I told Jill Kohlberg you'd ride with her

and Todd. The fewer cars parked nearby, the easier it will be to hide them from Devan."

Ricky's eyes open wide. "Shit-pants Todd."

"The man is about done with his MBA, cut him some slack."

"Um, what about Marilyn?" he asks. "Aren't she and Jill, like, connected at the hip."

"Yeah," I say, unsure why that's an issue. "She'll ride with the three of you too."

"Okay, I'm going to pass on the kid table...I mean car...whatever." Ricky sucks in a deep breath. "I'll ride with the Richardses."

"Kandace is going to meet us afterward. She said she wants to be there when I ask the question, but Dax is overprotective. Something about his ready-to-pop wife on an icy limestone ledge."

"Are you saying it'll be me and...Devan's friends?"

"No," I explain. "Dax, Cory, Mick, and Galvin are riding together. Kandace, Judy, and Chloe will be meeting us at Decoy Ducks. That's why it makes sense for you to ride with the girls."

"And Shit Pants." He grunts. "Devan better say yes."

My smile begins to curl. "I sure hope so. I mean, it's kind of soon, but with the farm...it seems right."

"Fine, what time is this going down?"

"Saturday at five, just in time for sunset."

A little backstory.

Jack and Janet Dunn took Dad's and my offer. In a few weeks, Ricky is moving to Bloomington to work on a bachelor's degree in accounting. He promises he'll still come around on the weekends to help out when I need him.

Jack and Janet found a home on the west coast of Florida, some small town that is still a fishing village. They plan to live between there and Riverbend. Even though we didn't tell them when they had to vacate the house on the new, larger Sheers farm, Devan said they are looking at smaller houses in town—something with less upkeep.

Now that Dad and I own what was the Dunn farm, the idea of moving out of my parents' home has dominated my thoughts—well, other than Devan. She's my number-one thought and the biggest reason it's time to move out. That is why I have a diamond solitaire in the pocket of my jeans. Classes finished up today for the holiday break.

In Riverbend, it's difficult to keep anything a secret, but I've done my best. My parents and Devan's parents know my plan. Jack and I had a long talk. I did the traditional thing, asking for his daughter's hand, telling him how much I love her and will work to take care of her. Mostly, I want to be a partner with her. I want the two of us to strive to make one another's dreams come true. He said I have his and Janet's blessings, but the decision is Devan's.

Saturday night, driving up to the farmhouse where the Dunns still live, I pat my pocket. If I hadn't told half of Riverbend to be at Empire Quarry, I could let my nerves get the better of me. A year ago, I couldn't have imagined proposing to anyone. As I get out of the truck and head toward the back door, I know I can't imagine living without Devan.

Once inside, I rub my hands together.

"Hi," Devan says, all smiles as she reaches for my hands. "You're cold."

"Yeah, it's cold out there." I scan her up and down, seeing her boots, blue jeans, and soft pink sweater. Higher still is her radiant smile, sexy soft-brown eyes, and her crown of yellow hair. "Are you ready?"

"Where are we going that I need to be bundled up?"

"It's a surprise." I turn up my smile. "Miss Dunn, you've just completed your first semester of teaching. I won't let that momentous occasion pass without a celebration."

"And we can't celebrate someplace warm?"

Seizing her chin, I bring her lips to mine. "I'll keep you warm."

Her orbs soften to a plush suede. "Now who could turn down that offer?"

As we drive, I talk about things to keep her distracted. It's when I stop the truck that Devan realizes where we are.

"Empire Quarry?"

"It's the first stop of our celebration."

After pulling a hat over her head, Devan pushes her hands into her gloves. "I'm glad you told me to be prepared."

The cold winter wind whips around, blowing a dusting of snow over the frozen ground. The green leaves are gone, and the bare branches of deciduous trees creak high above. Thankfully, the sun shone today, although it's about ready to set. The sky is filled with blues and grays. By the time we near the limestone ledge, my cheeks are cold, and Devan's are pink just like her nose.

I say a little prayer that everyone is set.

Stepping beyond the trees, the wind picks up and Devan wraps her arms around herself.

"I know it's cold," I say. "I could have waited until spring."

Her shimmering stare looks up at me. "Waited for what?"

Taking her hand, I fall to one knee.

"Oh, Justin."

"Devan, I told you that when I proposed marriage, you'd know it. That's what I want to do today." I look around. "In the cold, where we had our first date." With the darkening sky, I make out the silhouettes of our friends and family in the trees behind Devan. Looking up, I catch sight of a tear sliding down Devan's cheek. "I planned on staying a bachelor forever—not planned but was ready to. That life was easy and comfortable. And then one night when I least expected it, I came across a beautiful woman who took my breath away. She was everything I didn't know I was missing. From her sexy, confident banter to her earth-quaking kiss, I was blown away. The thing was, she wouldn't give me her name."

Devan's smile grows as more tears stream down her cheeks.

"And then I saw her again. There was every reason for me to stay away from her, but I couldn't. I knew after one kiss, Devan Dunn, you were meant to be mine and I yours. I know this is love because it's so damn strong that I want to be at your side for the rest of our lives. I love you more than I imagined I was capable of loving. Will you marry me?"

I pull the diamond from my pocket.

She nods quickly. "I love you too. Yes," she answers, falling to her knees and wrapping her arms around my neck.

As I tug her glove from her hand, a roar of applause erupts behind her.

Devan spins around and gasps as Ricky, Marilyn, Jill, Todd, Dax, Cory, Mick, Galvin, and Nick all come rushing out of the tree line.

Tugging on Devan's hand, I bring her attention back to me. "The ring?"

She nods as I slip the diamond solitaire onto her fourth finger.

"It's official. You're mine."

Her stunning smile grows. "And you're mine."

There are congratulations all around as the air fills with puffs of condensation, and we're surrounded.

Ricky slaps my shoulder. "So, what? You're a romantic now?"

I scoff.

"I'm just glad she didn't embarrass your ass in front of half of Riverbend."

It's not quite half but seeing the happy faces of our friends and family, I'm glad Devan said yes. Holding onto my arm, Devan smiles at me and her brother.

"Me too," I say, dropping a kiss on Devan's forehead.

Ricky goes on, "Seriously, let's take this party back to Decoy Ducks." He lifts his chin toward our friends and family. "We're all freezing."

"We're both going to be married." I hear Jill say to Devan as she reaches for her hand and looks at the ring.

"I'm officially a maid of honor for life," Marilyn responds.

Taking Devan's hand, I announce, "Dinner and drinks on me at Decoy Ducks."

"We all witnessed it," Ricky says, "miracles do happen. My sister accepted this guy's proposal, and he's going to buy."

Our friends laugh and cheer.

Epilogue

Justin
Six months later

One kiss.

It's what I'm thinking about as all the eyes of Riverbend are focused on me. I'm not being paranoid. I'm not climbing the metal bleachers to kiss my girl. Their eyes are on me because with Ricky at my side and Dax beside him, we're standing in the front of the church, wearing tuxedo pants, starched, itchy white shirts, bowties, and suspenders. I know I won't have their attention long because the music has started.

Jill is the first to come up the aisle. Marilyn is the next. The last is Molly in her flower-girl dress, a miniature version of Devan's from what I've gleaned. With her giant front teeth, Molly is all smiles as she drops a petal, steps, drops a petal. I'm currently cursing my sister for teaching Molly to move at a snail's pace, but I can't deny my niece is adorable. For the record, so is my second niece —Ruthie, named after Dax's grandma, the woman responsible for getting his head out of his ass.

Some people say the flower girl can steal the wedding.

My mouth goes dry as the congregation stands, and the doors at the back of the aisle open.

On Jack's arm, Devan is a showstopper.

Her radiant smile, the one I fell in love with over a year ago, is beaming up at me. If I'm supposed to notice the long white dress or anything about it, I'm failing because I can't wrench my gaze away from Devan's beautiful face.

Stunning.

Gorgeous.

I can't find words to describe what I see or how I feel.

The rumors around town are true. Miss Dunn will not be back next year teaching seventh-grade science. Mrs. Sheers will.

After Ricky moved to Bloomington for the second semester, Jack and Janet Dunn purchased a two-bedroom home in Riverbend. Their plan is to divide their time between here and Florida.

Of course, Devan and I told them they could always stay out at the farm—at *our* farm in *our* house, *our* home. Janet said she wanted us to make it our own, and we couldn't do that with them living there, even part time.

Once school released for the summer, Devan and I

went to work. We are tearing out walls and remodeling the kitchen. At first, I was afraid to change Devan's childhood home, but she reminded me she's no longer a child.

Ricky nudges me with his shoulder, bringing me to the present—to our wedding.

I take a step toward Devan.

Jack places Devan's hand in mine.

Seeing it there—in my grasp—I know without a doubt that holding her, touching her, and being with her is where I'm meant to be.

The wedding proceeds. I remember to place the wedding ring on her finger, and when I'm given permission, I lean in. "One kiss," I whisper.

After more photos than anyone should take are completed, I'm finally sitting at Devan's side. The reception is in full swing. Ricky and Marilyn have given their speeches. To be honest, it's mostly a blur. Until what happens next.

It's the part I'll never forget.

Devan leans close and whispers, "I have a surprise for you."

"Are you going to get me out of here early?"

"No," she says with a grin. "Just know when we're done" —her whisper grows lower— "I forgot to wear panties."

My eyes widen, and I lift my hand. "Check please."

And they lived happily ever after

Thank you for reading ONE KISS, Justin and Devan's story. If you enjoyed a visit to Riverbend, Indiana, check out Kandace and Dax's story, **QUINTESSENTIALLY THE ONE.**

All of Aleatha's lighter ones are stand-alone, steamy contemporary romances. Enjoy them all, free to read on Kindle Unlimited.

The Riverbend romances continue.

Turn the page to read about ONE STRING, coming in 2024, part of Aleatha's Lighter Ones—Ricky and Marilyn's story, a second-chance, enemies-to-lovers, little-sister's-best-friend, forbidden contemporary Riverbend romance.

Pre-order ONE STRING on all sales channels today. Upon release, ONE STRING will only be available to read for free in Kindle Unlimited.

<h1 style="text-align:center">One String</h1>

Second-chance, enemies-to-lovers, fake-date, little-sister's-best-friend, forbidden, stand-alone contemporary romance.

Ricky Dunn is the equivalent to a splinter under my fingernail.

Romantic?

Right.

He's the older brother of my best friend, and no matter how hard either of us try, we can't seem to avoid each other. The problem started on the night my best friend and I graduated from high school. The party was joyous, a celebration.

That night, I willingly gave Ricky a part of me—more than the kiss we told others about.

Our deal was simple.

No strings.

Ricky kept his side of the bargain.

Years have passed.

Being from the same small town and crossing paths, I haven't noticed how handsome he's become or the way he's filled out.

If you ask me, he hasn't noticed me either.

Until he calls.

I'm working for a finance company, one he's now interviewing for.

"Marilyn, will you be my date for the dinner with the partners? It's only for one date and no strings."

The problem is my heart hasn't kept my side of our bargain.

I want at least one string.

Do I agree to his proposal, or do I turn him down flat?

Have you been Aleatha'd?

Check out Aleatha's 2024 Lighter One—ONE STRING—second-chance, enemies-to-lovers, fake-date, little-sister's-best-friend, forbidden, stand-alone contemporary romance.

What to do now

LEND IT: Did you enjoy ONE KISS? Do you have a friend who'd enjoy ONE KISS? ONE KISS may be lent one time. Sharing is caring!

RECOMMEND IT: Do you have multiple friends who'd enjoy my lighter contemporary romance? Tell them about it! Call, text, post, tweet...your recommendation is the nicest gift you can give to an author!

REVIEW IT: Tell the world. Please go to the retailer where you purchased this book, as well as Goodreads, and write a review. Please share your thoughts about ONE KISS on:

*Amazon, ONE KISS Customer Reviews

*Barnes & Noble, ONE KISS, Customer Reviews

*Apple Books, ONE KISS Customer Reviews

* BookBub, ONE KISS Customer Reviews

*Goodreads.com/Aleatha Romig

ALL AVAILABLE TO READ ON KINDLE UNLIMITED

ROYAL REFLECTIONS SERIES:

RUTHLESS REIGN

November 2022

RESILIENT REIGN

January 2023

RAVISHING REIGN

April 2023

RELEVANT REIGN

June 2023

READY TO BINGE:

SIN SERIES:

RED SIN

October 2021

GREEN ENVY

January 2022

GOLD LUST

April 2022

BLACK KNIGHT

June 2022

STAND-ALONE ROMANTIC SUSPENSE:

SILVER LINING

October 2022

KINGDOM COME

November 2021

DEVIL'S SERIES (Duet):

DEVIL'S DEAL

May 2021

ANGEL'S PROMISE

June 2021

WEB OF SIN:

SECRETS

October 2018

LIES

December 2018

PROMISES

January 2019

TANGLED WEB:

TWISTED

May 2019

OBSESSED

July 2019

BOUND

August 2019

WEB OF DESIRE:

SPARK

Jan. 14, 2020

FLAME

February 25, 2020

ASHES

April 7, 2020

DANGEROUS WEB:

Prequel: "Danger's First Kiss"

DUSK

November 2020

DARK

January 2021

DAWN

February 2021

* * *

THE INFIDELITY SERIES:

BETRAYAL

Book #1

October 2015

CUNNING

Book #2

January 2016

DECEPTION

Book #3

May 2016

ENTRAPMENT

Book #4

September 2016

FIDELITY

Book #5

January 2017

* * *

THE CONSEQUENCES SERIES:

CONSEQUENCES

(Book #1)

August 2011

TRUTH

(Book #2)

October 2012

CONVICTED

(Book #3)

October 2013

REVEALED

(Book #4)

Previously titled: Behind His Eyes Convicted: The Missing
Years

June 2014

BEYOND THE CONSEQUENCES

(Book #5)

January 2015

RIPPLES (Consequences stand-alone)

October 2017

CONSEQUENCES COMPANION READS:

BEHIND HIS EYES-CONSEQUENCES

January 2014

BEHIND HIS EYES-TRUTH

March 2014

* * *

STAND ALONE MAFIA THRILLER:

PRICE OF HONOR

Available Now

* * *

STAND-ALONE ROMANTIC THRILLER:

ON THE EDGE

May 2022

***

Stand-alone fun, sexy romance

May 2018

ONE NIGHT

Stand-alone, sexy contemporary romance

September 2017

A SECRET ONE

April 2018

MY ALWAYS ONE

Stand-Alone, sexy friends to lovers contemporary romance

July 2021

QUINTESSENTIALLY THE ONE

Stand-alone, small-town, second-chance, secret baby contemporary romance

July 2022

MY ONLY ONE

Stand-alone, small-town, best friend's sister, grump/sunshine contemporary romance.

July 2023

* * *

INDULGENCE SERIES:

UNEXPECTED

August 2018

UNCONVENTIONAL

January 2018

UNFORGETTABLE

October 2019

UNDENIABLE

August 2020

ABOUT THE AUTHOR

Aleatha Romig is a New York Times, Wall Street Journal, and USA Today bestselling author who lives in Indiana, USA. She has raised three children with her high school sweetheart and husband of over thirty years. Before she became a full-time author, she worked days as a dental hygienist and spent her nights writing. Now, when she's not imagining mind-blowing twists and turns, she likes to spend her time with her family and friends. Her other pastimes include reading and creating heroes/anti-heroes who haunt your dreams!

Aleatha impresses with her versatility in writing. She released her first novel, CONSEQUENCES, in August of 2011. CONSEQUENCES, a dark romance, became a bestselling series with five novels and two companions released from 2011 through 2015. The compelling and epic story of Anthony and Claire Rawlings has graced more than half a million e-readers. Her first stand-alone smart, sexy thriller INSIDIOUS was next. Then Aleatha released the five-novel INFIDELITY series, a romantic suspense saga, that took the reading world by storm, the final book landing on three of the top bestseller lists. She ventured into traditional publishing with Thomas and Mercer. Her books INTO THE LIGHT and AWAY

FROM THE DARK were published through this mystery/thriller publisher in 2016.

In the spring of 2017, Aleatha again ventured into a different genre with her first fun and sexy stand-alone romantic comedy with the USA Today bestseller PLUS ONE. She continued the "Ones" series with additional standalones, ONE NIGHT, ANOTHER ONE, MY ALWAYS ONE, and QUINTESSENTIALLY THE ONE. If you like fun, sexy, novellas that make your heart pound, try her "Indulgence series" with UNCONVEN-TIONAL. UNEXPECTED, UNFORGETTABLE, and UNDENIABLE.

In 2018 Aleatha returned to her dark romance roots with SPARROW WEBS. And continued with the mafia romance DEVIL'S DUET, and most recently her SIN series.

You may find all Aleatha's titles on her website.

Aleatha is a "Published Author's Network" member of the Romance Writers of America and PEN America. She is represented by Kevan Lyon of Marsal Lyon Literary Agency and Dani Sanchez with Wildfire Marketing.

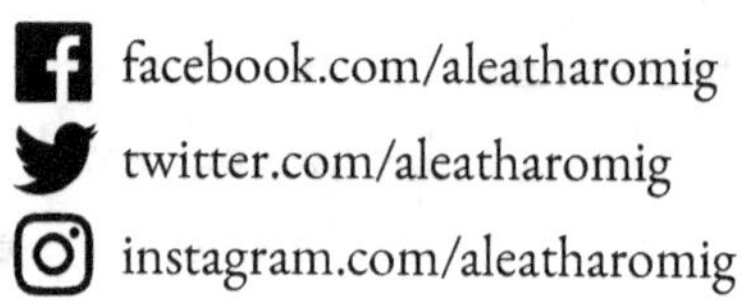

facebook.com/aleatharomig

twitter.com/aleatharomig

instagram.com/aleatharomig